AT THIS JUNCTURE

ALSO BY RONA ALTROWS

A Run on Hose
Key in Lock
Shy (ed., with Naomi K. Lewis)
The River Throws a Tantrum (children's chapbook,
illustrated by Sarah-joy Geddes)

AT THIS JUNCTURE

A Book of Letters

RONA ALTROWS

| N₁ | O₂ | N₁ |

CANADA

*Publisher's note: This book is a work of fiction. Names, characters, places and incidents are
either the product of the author's imagination or are used fictitiously. Some characters are
based on living or dead persons, but the views those characters express do not necessarily
represent the views of the persons on whom the characters are based.*

Library and Archives Canada Cataloguing in Publication

Altrows, Rona, 1948–, author
At this juncture : a book of letters / Rona Altrows.

ISBN 978–1–988098–46–3 (softcover)

I. Title.

PS8601.L87A8 2018   C813'.6   C2018–900454–1

Printed and bound in Canada on 100% recycled paper.

Now Or Never Publishing
901, 163 Street
Surrey, British Columbia
Canada V4A 9T8

nonpublishing.com
Fighting Words.

We gratefully acknowledge the support of the Canada Council for the Arts
and the British Columbia Arts Council for our publishing program.

For Bill

And in memory of my parents, Hyman and Rae Altrows

Contents

First letter to the CEO of Canada Post

December 12, 2013

Dear Mr. Chopra,

Yesterday I learned to my dismay that Canada Post has continued to suffer great losses. One need not be an economic analyst to realize that extensive use of the Internet has been a major cause of the decline of our postal service. The news that Canada Post did not do well over the past year did not come as a surprise to me and I am sure you were not flabbergasted either.

According to the news stories, Canada Post will rely largely on parcel delivery for its revenue in future. Good luck with that, as you attempt to run head to head against the Amazonian drones that will be sharing our air space before you know it.

I have a proposal. It will not cost much, and I am confident it will breathe life into your moribund letter delivery service. It is true, I am not a corporate consultant by profession; I am an just an ordinary woman in my fifties with wide interests but no particular expertise in business. However, I do have a passion that I am willing to share, and if you will only let me do so, I will show you a way to get Canada Post back in the black.

You see, Mr. Chopra, I pride myself on being a dedicated writer of letters. At the age of six, I wrote my first letter. It was to my aunt Bella, who resided in Moosomin, Saskatchewan. Aunt Bella and I carried on a lively correspondence until her death twenty-three years later. Each of us wrote the other a minimum of once a week and our letters always travelled by mail. Therefore, in the course of the years we were in postal contact, we purchased, by my calculation, at least 2,392 Canadian stamps. I think it can fairly be said Aunt Bella and I did our share to keep our country's postal service profitable.

Through that rewarding experience with my aunt, I discovered early in life the power and beauty of letter writing and letter reading. Today, although it would be quicker, cheaper, and more efficient to send e-mails or communicate over social media, I still write and mail numerous letters to friends all over the world. Consequently, I still buy many stamps.

Regrettably, I cannot single-handedly keep my favourite Crown corporation afloat. I can, however, volunteer some of my time (although if you think it appropriate, you might wish to offer me an honourarium) to do something that may change Canada Post into a happy corporation once again.

You see, I love to read about the achievements of people from all periods of human history, and, for my own amusement, I write ersatz historical letters. I have created quite a collection of phony yet credible letters—from historical people to other historical people, from historical people to people I made up in my head, from people I made up in my head to historical people, and so on. I can share these letters with you, so that you can make them available to the people of Canada—but only if they buy stamps. So if someone buys, say, a package of ten stamps, she or he gets to read the fake letter from General James Wolfe's last letter to his mother. For a purchase of twenty stamps, the reward is the fake letter from Karl Marx's wife to his cousin. My fabricated letters respect history—I am careful about that—but at the same time, they add quite a bit of feasible, sometimes juicy speculation. Some of the subjects of my letters are lesser known than others, and so may pique the curiosity of customers who prefer the obscure. And purchasers already sold on the letters to do with the more famous subjects may wish to look further.

But what of the prospective stamp purchasers who are not history or biography buffs? What is their epistolary incentive for buying stamps? Well, they may be drawn to letters I have written, as a concerned consumer, to businesses whose performance has been less than stellar. (Naturally, when I write any such letter I go to the local stationers' store and make a copy on the DIY xerox machine for five cents a page. Hence, I have copies of all such letters and can give you the best for our sales-incentive line.)

I have changed all company names and locations, liability issues being what they are.

And yes, I will share some of my personal correspondence too, knowing full well that some customers are going to be most drawn in by letters that are contemporary. I have checked with my best friend Leo Ellison, who is in his early twenties and figures prominently in the letters I will share with you and you will share with Canada. It is possible there will be repercussions from Leo's mother. However, I am accustomed to dealing with her rancour and I can assure you, Canada Post will suffer no harm at her hands. I am her sole target.

Doesn't my scheme make eminent sense? You see the hook. Reading letters makes people want to write their own letters, more and more of them, and send them all by post. And for that, they need stamps.

Ironically, you may wish to make use of the Internet as one means of advertising the existence of my letters to stamp purchasers. If you need any assistance in wending your way through the world of electronic communication, we can bring Leo in as a consultant. He is extremely knowledgeable in such matters— more savvy, I would venture to say, than even most of his own technologically sophisticated cohort, Generation Screwed.

I am confident that within a month of disseminating my letters as rewards, you will note a surge in sales of what you term on your website "lettermail" stamps. Soon, the entire nation will be writing letters in surging numbers. You will have buy-in from across the country. Your revenues will soar. And who can even calculate the potential goodwill our program will generate?

We all want Canada Post to do well, Mr. Chopra. Let me help you make that happen.

Sincerely,
Ariadne Jensen

p.s. Here is another promotional idea, one that has just occurred to me. I am sure your personal office is quite large. If you can find a corner for me, and provide me with a notepad, I will write a series of letters, targeted to different readers, about the value of letter writing. There can be one letter for young children just learning to read and write, one for older children, one for teenagers, one for millennials, one for GenExers, one for Gen Ys, and so forth. Even though I have not quite reached that point in my life, I am sure I can fashion good letters for the so-called young-old in their sixties and early seventies and another for more senior seniors. (Mind you, I am not too sure older people need as much convincing about the virtues of letter writing, something they grew up with.) What do you think?

Second letter to the CEO of Canada Post

May 27, 2015

Dear Mr. Chopra,

How I wish you had heeded the advice I offered you in my letter of December 12, 2013. Now see what has happened? Canada Post's money problems have gotten worse. So unnecessary.

There has been an eight percent decline in lettermail volume so far this year, and you have put the blame squarely on Canadians, saying we have abandoned our "social contract" with Canada Post. The lifestyle of Canadians is digital, you observe. Does that surprise you? Look around. We live in a digital world. What are we Canadians supposed to do? Withdraw from the rest of the planet? Move Canada to Mars?

The Canadian public is not the culprit, Mr. Chopra. And for heaven's sake, do not raise postage again, as you say you are about to do. That will only deter people further. If you want us to use the mail service, make the extra effort worth our while.

Have you noticed that internationally, the letter is making a comeback? Even on the Internet, an increasing number of websites are devoted, perhaps ironically, to letters—real letters, fictional letters, the changing physical appearance of letters, the history of letters, the role of letters in genealogical research. I could go on. This is a perfect time to revive the art of letter writing in Canada, and on a grand scale.

In spite of your failure to respond to my letter of December 12, 2013 (and only you know the reason for that non-response), I have forged ahead with my plans and now have even more letters, both ersatz and real, with which you can entice Canadians to buy large quantities of stamps. You may even want to offer discount prices. Volume—that is the key. A high volume of stamp sales will restore financial health to our much beloved postal corporation.

As a further sales stimulus, I have grouped the letters into bundles, with written comments to go with every bundle. You can use those comments as marketing hooks, both in print ads and on the evil interwebs.

As more people buy stamps and therefore read more of my letters, and as they are prompted to write more letters of their own, you will become aware of beneficial side effects. Excited by the innate value of the letter, more people will want to work for Canada Post. And indeed, there will be a place in the corporation for all of them, since we will need more letter carriers to deliver the letters Canadians will be writing in ever greater numbers. You will therefore acquire more contributors to your pension plan and, in the fullness of time, you will eliminate its deficit. I know we are talking about close to seven billion dollars, but really, Mr. Chopra, one must start somewhere.

There is no more time to lose. Let us work together to save Canada Post. I await your prompt reply.

Sincerely,
Ariadne Jensen

p.s. Since you have been silent on the matter of offering me temporary office space (and on all other matters), I have abandoned the plan to write demographically targeted pitches. If you consider those pitches critical to the success of our plan, we can renegotiate next week when you respond.

A HUNDRED THOUSAND BEATS

atria, ventricles, valves
aorta, pulmonary artery
superior vena cava
inferior vena cava
conduction
circulation

fist-sized muscle
a hundred thousand beats a day
the human heart works hard

fall for a politician, hard
fall for a poet, harder
find the one, soon snatched
live as a sentient statue, no right to love

the busy heart never stops,
damaged or not

AJ

TO SOPHIE MARX FROM JENNY MARX

64 Dean Street
Soho
London
October 4, 1851

Dearest Sophie,
A personal matter has been weighing heavily on my heart, so much
so I have come to realize I must unburden myself or I may lose my
senses, and you, my sweet sister-in-law and best friend of my childhood, are the one in whom I have resolved to place my trust.
Although Karl's exile, the demands of the work we insist upon
doing in spite of the many attendant dangers, and, above all, family
responsibilities have kept me from being a frequent correspondent
with you in recent years, I will cherish forever the closeness we
enjoyed as girls growing up in Trier. You will always have my
deepest gratitude for having introduced me to your younger
brother and also for having kept faith as our sole confidante when
Karl and I were not yet in a position to disclose our engagement
to the rest of the world. I do not exaggerate when I tell you that
without my little wild boar Karl, I would be unable to carry on.

How, then, could the events I am about to describe possibly
have occurred? I myself am at a loss to understand, much less
interpret rationally, what has happened, nor can I predict with
any certainty how the consequences of those recent events may
affect our future.

Last year, owing to the exigencies of life and the repeated
failure of publishers to pay Karl his due for articles and essays, we
amassed tremendous debt, to the point that I feared we would
starve and face eviction from our small flat here in Soho. I saw
no means of continuing to support Jennychen, Laura, our

comical Edgar and poor baby Fawksy, who had been sickly from
the first. How were our children to live?

By day, Karl retreated to the library of the British Museum to
write; by night he led discussions on politics and society with his
fellow thinkers, writers and activists over cigars and beer. It fell
upon my shoulders to attend to our practical crisis, or so I felt. It
embarrasses and pains me to admit this to you, but I saw no solu-
tion except to ask your wealthy uncle Lion Philips in Holland for
help. After a turbulent voyage, during which I suffered from
severe *mal de mer*, I finally arrived at Lion's home in Zaltbommel
to an icy reception, a flat refusal of money, and an unsolicited
suggestion that I leave my husband. In consequence I departed
immediately, in a wretched and defeated state of mind. My one
solace was the knowledge that in my absence, Lenchen had been
caring for the children and Karl. Yes, Helene "Lenchen" Demuth
still manages our household. Who better to help tend to the needs
of my children than Lenchen—a woman who has been in the
service of my family of birth, the Westphalens, since her own
childhood. Six years ago my mother sent Lenchen from Trier to
work for Karl and me and she has been with us since, becoming
in our minds and hearts a member of the Marx family and stoically
enduring with us the privations to which we have been subjected—our punishment by society as a result of Karl's critical work.

I learned during my trip that I was once again pregnant;
however, some months after my return, it became obvious that
Lenchen was also expecting a baby. How could that be, since she
was in our home day and night, except to go out on errands?

She did not speak of the matter. None of us did. I had the
distinct feeling that Karl was ill at ease: I would need to repeat
the simplest request to him two or three times before he even
became aware that I was talking to him and he retreated to the
library even more than usual. While I dreaded learning the truth,
I simultaneously became less and less able to bear the uncertainty,
and finally decided I must ask Karl directly. *He will assure me it is
not so*, I told myself. *He will say the child Lenchen carries was fathered
by Friedrich Engels. After all, Mr. Engels was our house guest at the
time Lenchen must have conceived, and Engels and Lenchen are fond*

enough of each other. Alas, no. Karl cried like a child and confessed; he placed the blame on a transitory weakness brought on by alcohol, loneliness in my absence, and the worst imaginable luck, since there had been only one brief encounter. I was unmoved by the tears of my little wild boar. I felt only revulsion.

Since then I cannot begin to describe to you the extent of my mental turmoil.

Our Franziska was born on March 28 of this year. In the summer Lenchen gave birth. A boy. She gave him up to a family in August; I know nothing of the arrangements she may have made to see her son, nor do I have any inclination to inquire. Lenchen continues to live with Karl and me and our children as though our household were under no strain. I have never spoken to her of her act of indiscretion with my husband. Karl does not talk of it, of course; indeed, he must hope I lose interest in the sordid liaison. He must wish that eventually all knowledge of it be erased from my memory.

The truth is I share that wish. How many more nights can I spend weeping and how many more days can I spend desiring to inflict some ill-defined harm on Lenchen, manager of my household, caretaker of my little ones, companion of mine since our youth? How long can I remain deeply distrustful of my beloved husband, the centre of my life? Karl and I and Lenchen all need one another.

It is my hope, dearest Sophie, that by telling you what has happened, I can finally relieve myself of resentment and suspicion, if not of secrecy. I put my trust in you without any condition or reservation, for I know you will keep this matter in complete confidence. If it were ever to come to light in my lifetime, the shame would destroy me and much more importantly, the information could cause incalculable damage to Karl's work.

I hope you and Mr. Schmalhausen are in the best of health and spirits and that you and I will see each other again at a time of far greater tranquillity.

Yours ever,
Jenny Marx

To John A. Macdonald from Elizabeth Hall

Peterborough
Province of Canada
17 April, 1859

Loved John,

How I miss your company, your laugh, your quaint vests.

As it has now been a week since your last visit and you tell me in your last letter it will be a fortnight before you can come again, I have turned my mind to contemplation of what has occurred between us and what may come to pass in the days ahead.

I must say once again how grateful I am for all your assistance after what happened to George last year. One does not expect a man in his thirty-ninth year—a judge, once a politician, filled with vitality and ambition—to die. What fun you and George must have had together in Montreal during the 'forties when you served the Conservative cause together at the Legislative Assembly. George spoke to me often about your camaraderie at that time, not just as colleagues but as warm friends. It is a testimonial to the strength of your friendship that it continued right until his death. I have said this to you many times before, I know—forgive me, but I simply must restate—it meant a great deal to me when you undertook to administer George's estate and to set up the trust funds for the children. How magnanimous of you to relieve me of those practical burdens in that wretched period.

You have done no wrong in visiting me openly in recent months. Why should you not, when there is nothing to hide? Nevertheless, a number of the fine folk of Peterborough, whom I shall not name here but whose identities you will, no doubt, arrive at through conjecture, have decided that our affairs are theirs. They speak in excited half-whispers, loudly enough for me to know they are talking about us, yet softly enough for me not to hear the entirety of their remarks. I cannot fathom the cause of their agitation. Surely it is normal and proper for two souls who are friends to intensify their relations when they both find themselves without mates.

But oh, Peterborough's protectors of propriety say, Mrs. Hall is just past a year a widow; moreover, is it not unseemly for the premier to be spending time with any lady so soon after his wife's demise? Why, she has only been gone since the winter of '57.

And I inquire in return, is that not long enough for a vigorous man to grieve?

In any case, how little the righteous of Peterborough understand the patience with which you endured the demands placed on you by Isabella's strange and mysterious illness, which no physician could ever identify, yet which rendered her an invalid for almost the whole fourteen years of your marriage. And all the while you were seeing to the well-being of your mother and sisters as well. Those trips to the United States to allow her to visit her sisters must have been a trial for both you and Isabella, with her always being so unwell. I am glad she had the benefit of comforting medicines—Godfrey's Cordial, McMunn's Elixir of Opium and the finest brand of laudanum, Mother's Quietness. And when consumption set in, were you not the most generous of husbands? When the end drew nigh, did you not rush from Toronto to Kingston on Christmas Day and sit vigil by her bedside for three days until she slipped away?

As concerns past loves, I say you have done your duty and I, mine. May the tongues of the pious of Peterborough fall out of their mouths, for they have no conception of what I have with you. It is nothing they will allow themselves, even with their own husbands.

At the same time, more generous souls here have engaged in their own kind of speculation. These gentler people talk to me directly. "You are still quite young," they tell me, "your waist is still as narrow as if you had never borne children, your features are pleasant, your spirit is strong. What an asset you would be to a politician with burning drive, as you were to your late husband, may he rest in eternal peace."

Take what you will from what the kinder folk tell me. I am pleased to report their comments. Meanwhile, until the future is settled, I hope I bring you some combination of respite and pleasure.

Goodbye until the next time, my dear one.

Love,
Your darling Lizzie

To Peter Fagan from Helen Keller

February 5, 1917

Dear Peter,
This will be my last letter.

I need to do all I can to win back the trust of my mother, who does not know we have been corresponding.

You know how she reacted in the fall when she discovered our engagement through that awful article in the Globe. "That animal," she called you. Her feelings have not changed. She is convinced you are a user who would have tried to exploit me by gaining access to famous people. Aware of your friendship with John Reed, your admiration of Emma Goldman and your opposition to the war, she was also afraid you would turn me into a radical.

So she said. But she knew, as everyone did, that I was already a committed socialist before we met; had written *Out of the Dark*; had made many anti-war speeches and statements of my own, and not just on the Chautauqua tours.

Her real reason for intercepting us was simply this: you are a man, and one who sees me as a woman. My mother and my teacher Mrs. Macy both believe there must be no such man for me. I am expected to set aside, for my whole life, all romantic and sexual urges. I am to be pure, three-sensed Helen, not a woman with normal desires but a mobile statue, representing nobility of spirit and selflessness.

It is lucky my mother cannot unlock my head at night and gain entry to my dreams. I can hardly imagine how shocked she would be.

Nevertheless, her actions are driven by love and worry for me, and I still feel sorrow for the way I behaved toward her at the time you and I planned our elopement. I was afraid she would ruin everything for us and of course, that is what she eventually did. But I had never been dishonest with her before, it put me into panic to deny the truth, and don't think I could lie to her again, no matter what the reason.

Silence brings no peace to a deaf-blind child; it only cuts her off inhumanly from others and self. Where would I have been, how would I have ended up, without my mother's work to find me help? How would I have met my teacher when I was seven, and what would I understand of this world today? Were it not for my mother's efforts, and the arrival of Teacher, I would still be a phantom creature, existing in a time that had neither night nor day, and with only the most rudimentary consciousness, not even amounting to self-awareness.

When I was just out of my freshman year at Radcliffe, Dr. Bell, who is like a grandfather to me, invited me to his summer home in Cape Breton and talked to me in private, to explore my thoughts on love and marriage. He did not feel I should deprive myself forever. He wanted me to open my heart and mind to the possibility of some day becoming someone's wife.

But, like my mother, Teacher has always said I should redirect my womanly urges. There is no place in my life for such nonsense, she says. Inevitably men deceive, she says (perhaps because she is so hurt, with her own marriage to John Macy having come to a bitter end). I should channel all my passion— of every kind—into my advocacy for the blind and deaf, my speaking engagements, my writings, my unofficial ambassadorship for all those who are different. Sink all that energy into the work, Teacher says.

I lied to Teacher too, about you and me. Now she puts up with my corresponding with you only because she knows that I intend to say goodbye to you forever, and she does not want me to fret, in future years, over things not said.

Still, I am human, and although I do not intend to have another adventure like ours, I will not forget it.

Of our time as a couple, the greatest joy for me came at the very start, last September. I was sitting in my study by myself, feeling utterly isolated and dejected, when you came in and took my hand. How I savoured our long silence, so different from the silence caused by missing a sense. The silence of you and me filled me up. Finally you spelled your feelings into my hand. I sometimes say every atom in my body is a vibroscope. Never more than then. I had not felt your hand in mine before except through your work as my temporary secretary, filling in for Polly. Now, in the study, you touched me differently, spoke into my hand as a lover. Oh, I can read a hand. Our love was simple. No obstacles had been placed in our path. No lies had been told to others.

Perhaps I should have followed my own instinct, to tell Mother and Teacher right away of our plan to marry, but I listened to you when you said we should wait a little, to give you a chance to grow on them. And so began the secrecy, the deceit, the discoveries that led to the unravelling of our plans.

Suppose we had done as I wished? Is it possible, as I have speculated, that our concealment only thwarted our chances? What if we had been able to carry out our elopement plans? If the city clerk's office in Boston had not leaked to the press that we had applied for a marriage license. If my sister's husband Warren had not gone after you with a gun.

Had we been able to carry out our plan, would you and I have embarked upon a happy life together? Would I have been filled with contentment, as I was when you held my hand that night in the study? Or perhaps I would have been so distracted by love for you that I would have neglected my work.

Perhaps you would have become frustrated with helping me constantly, with the loss of opportunity to pursue your own career as a journalist. Or you, like Teacher, might have developed chronic headaches after nine hours in a row of reading me newspapers, mail, and books not available in Braille.

I do not think there is an unfolding or outcome I have not considered in my ruminations. In my mind, we have lived as man and wife. How does our life together play out? That depends on which of my daydreams we choose. Our marriage has been a haven, a catastrophe, an isle of contentment, a bog of frustration.

I have carried on these imaginings for a month more or less, and a strange thing has happened. My romantic feelings have dissipated. I could not go back to you now even if it were possible, for I am no longer at the same point as I was last fall.

Finally, at 37, I have come to understand on a deeper level that my mother and my teacher are right. I know what I must do, where I must put my all my stamina.

As to what passed between you and me personally, I regret nothing. But now it is over, and I must continue with my life's work. I hope you enjoy fulfillment as you forge ahead with your own life too. Please do not contact me again.

Goodbye,
Helen

To Ruth Draper from Amy Piperdale

Galt, Ontario
June 10, 1945

Dear Miss Draper,
For years I have been following your career. Finally my dream of seeing you live turned to reality: I was in your audience last spring in Montreal, when you performed your one-woman show at the hospital where my fiancé, Damien, was under treatment. "In a Church in Italy," what a drama. You portrayed—you *became*—to perfection, the pretentious artist, the earnest American tourist, the insistent beggar, the old woman immersed in supplication and prayer. And "Doctors and Diets," another gem. How we howled as your character, Mrs. Grimmer, rambled on about the hundred-lemon juice cure and the miraculous Vitamin Q that builds the brain. We loved it when she (you) exclaimed, "Here we are in the best restaurant in town and none of us can eat!" For us that mono-logue was darkly comical, as Damien was living on bland institu-tional food and, of course, in a medical setting.

So many personalities presented and so many others evoked over so short a time by one person on a virtually bare stage, with no props save a few hats and shawls—how do you do it? What I noticed in particular was the compassion in your voice and the depth of expression in your eyes, even at the funniest moments. I could have, should have, tried to meet you afterward, to thank you personally for the show. However, bashfulness held me back, as it so often does.

I know you are friends with old Miss Wilks, and have stayed with her here in Galt at her Cruickston Park property. I am positive you were here last April and I have been given to under-stand you were also here in '43. Perhaps it is a stretch to say Miss

Wilks is a link between you and me. She is a well-to-do heiress whereas I come from more common stock. But as it happens, my family hails from Galt too. You have been here, you have visited with someone in my community, so surely that counts for something in the way of connection between you and me.

To be honest, I look for connection with you wherever I can. It is true I keep track of your tours, your command performances for royal personages and so forth, but I have also read newspaper articles touching on your personal life, including the event of 1931 that brought such tragedy to you. I wept in sympathy with you then. And now, of all the people on this confusing planet, you may be the only one who can fully comprehend my state of mind, my constant preoccupation.

You see, like you, I found what the French call "l'amour de ma vie" long after I thought any such thing could happen. When I met Damien four years ago, I was already in my forties; he, in his late twenties. He had been rejected for military service because of a history of heart problems. We first came across each other on a Saturday morning at the Red Cross Office in Montreal; we were among the voluntary workers assembling food parcels to be sent overseas to Prisoners of War. Somehow our eyes met, first by accident, then by design. At the end of our volunteer shift he invited me out for a bite at the Woolworth's lunch counter on Ste. Catherine Street. The attention took me aback; I stumbled and stammered my way through a grilled cheese sandwich and strawberry ice cream soda. Undeterred by my reserve, Damien invited me out again. And again. I felt ever more at ease with him as time went on.

Damien made his living as an engineer for the Bell Telephone Company but his true calling was as a writer of stories—slice-of-life stories, vignettes. He never tried to get them published—he wrote purely for pleasure. He did let me read some of his pieces and I was much impressed. Was his work of as high a quality as that of your love, Lauro de Bosis? I am a simple secretary and it is not within my ability to judge (although Damien often told me I underestimated myself and had it in me to do more, perhaps attend university and become a professional person of some kind.) In my opinion, for whatever it may be worth, Damien's stories have power and beauty. Also delicious humour. When I first read them, my adoration for him grew.

For some reason, Damien found me fascinating. Once I became comfortable enough with him I was able to speak freely on many subjects. He called me an excellent conversationalist. I don't know about that, but as a result of his kind words, I did muster up the courage to take a night class in Public Speaking at my alma mater, the High School of Montreal. It is not something I would ever have considered doing before we met.

We travelled to Ottawa together, to Quebec City, to Vermont. We were both still living in Montreal but I brought him on holiday to Galt to introduce him to my family. And it was here, on a sultry August night, that he proposed. I was euphoric.

But soon after we returned to Montreal and resumed our jobs, he fell ill. It was his heart again. He made an admirable effort to keep working, to go on living normally, but his condition continued to deteriorate. In the springtime, he was hospitalized. During this worrying period, your performance brought us a moment of brightness, for which we were grateful.

The doctors said he was starting to improve. My hopes surged. But just before his scheduled release from hospital, Damien had a massive coronary. They could not save him. For a while my despair defined me. I continued to go to my job every day but my existence was hollow. I had to decide whether to live or die. In six months, and with some help from my doctor, I chose to go on living. The goal then became to return to full mental health, and so I came back to Galt, to be close to family and long-time friends, at least for a while. Then I had to figure out how best to honour the memory of Damien. And that is the question that occupies my mind now.

Your Lauro was a modern hero of sorts. I have learned about his work with the Alleanza Nazionale, his labours as a translator and of course, his poetry. Naturally I read about his fateful flight over Rome in October of '31, delivering anti-fascist pamphlets— the flight from which he never returned. I read in the newspaper

and cried with all the world a few days later over the testament
he had left, "The Story of My Death." Is it true you translated it
from the Italian? That must have been so difficult for you emo-
tionally. And you have done so much to keep his memory alive.
I have read your translation of his greatest work, the long poem
Icaro. But Lauro was an extraordinary man, Miss Draper, as you
are an extraordinary woman. I am ordinary; Damien, in the eyes
of all but me, perhaps, was ordinary.

Yet, perhaps his stories did set Damien apart from the mass
of men. Oh, they are good. I feel immersed in the scene as I read
them.

We knew his condition could be fatal and in his will, along
with a generous lump sum, he bequeathed all his notebooks to
me. I knew that gift was coming; we had discussed it. He had
told me he did not expect me to do anything with the notebooks;
he simply did not have the heart to have them thrown out. There
are many notebooks, filled with stories written over a twelve-
year period. It makes me sad to think that perhaps nobody else
will ever read Damien's literary pearls. Perhaps I could put
together a small collection of some kind and show it to a publisher. I have no idea how one goes about doing something like that.
Can you advise me?

Or perhaps I am being foolish. Thinking about the notebook
stories may just be another way to dwell on the past. It may be
best for me to store away the notebooks and get on with life.
Damien would not want me to be melancholy.

Whatever your advice, brava for your artistry. And thank
you for taking the time to listen to a woman who, like you, has
lost the love of her life.

Yours in admiration,
Amy Piperdale

To Rabindranath Tagore
from Anapurna Turkhud

January 19, 1879
Bombay, India

Dear Rabi,
Are you enjoying your first English winter? I hope you have secured a stout woolen topcoat as I suggested.

My family is also about to embark on a trip, but from west to east rather than the reverse—we leave shortly for Calcutta. It is not sure yet whether both my sisters will take the journey. Manik has a strong sense of adventure and wants to come, but Durga has asked my father if she can stay behind. "Baba," she told him, "I want to concentrate on my studies." Baba does not like to deny any of his daughters a reasonable request, so I think it likely only he and Manik and I will travel on this occasion.

Baba has arranged that while we are in the region, he will meet with your father at Jorasanko, and raise the subject of you and me—our possible future. Will your father be receptive to my father's proposition? Baba tries to prepare me for disappointment; he feels the Maharshi Debendranath Tagore may not be amenable. But I am more optimistic.

Away from you, my solace is that you are now where I spent several years of my own schooling, so I can see you, in my mind's eye, exploring central London or walking along the pebbled beach of Brighton. At the same time, Poet, I yearn for your return to India. Mentally I create, over and over, an ideal day with you here in Bombay. It is so like a typical day during the time your stay with us last year.

May I make a revelation to you? For the entire three months you were here, I wrote in a tablet every night before sleep. My words sometimes leaned toward the philosophical but often they were personal. Of course I wrote of you. Today, when my father was away, I put the tablet on his desk in his study, in the hope he will read at least some of my entries. My wish is to strengthen his resolve when he talks to the Maharshi Tagore.

My father's fear that his mission will fail stems mainly from the fact our family does not belong to Brahmo Samaj. Particularly because your father has been a leader in the revival of the Samaj, my father is afraid the barrier may be insurmountable. I, however, must continue to aspire to a life with you; else I will become despondent.

I have always considered myself a fortunate girl. How rare it is in our country for a father to insist upon the education of all his daughters, to send them all to England to broaden their cultural horizons, to encourage the development of their intellectual lives. Manik wishes to become a doctor; I wish to become a writer; Durga continues to search for the path of her choice. At every turn, Baba encourages us to pursue our studies and our dreams.

This year, I have been feeling particularly lucky, since Baba and your older brother Satyendranath are such good friends. I will always be grateful to Satyendranath for suggesting you come and stay with our family for a little while, as a stepping-stone to your travels abroad. I hope you feel you learned a little about how the English live, from the stories we told you. Certainly by the time you left your conversational English had improved greatly. You learn so quickly.

Why cannot our country be such that people may marry whom they wish, without considerations of sub-caste, family standing, religious inclination? My father has assured me he will tell your father he is sympathetic to many of Brahmo ideals, rooted as the Brahmo Sanjab is in the belief in only one god and, indeed, in the acceptance of religious pluralism. "But since that is so, Baba, won't the Maharshi be well-disposed to your request, and let the poet and me have our happiness?" I asked. "Not necessarily," he told me. "Tradition pulls hard."

Regardless of what the future holds, I am certain of one thing. When I have written essays good enough to publish, I will

go by the author name Nalini—the name you have given me and
have woven into your songs.

Farewell until the next time, Poet.
Your devoted Nalini

p.s. In a nightmare, I married a dour Scot and moved to
Edinburgh, where my life was porridge grey.

KIN

They assuage your pain, tear you up, keep you whole.
You want the best for them, you say. You know what that means, you think.
They've got you.
AJ

To her sister Hendrika from Helena Jans

Deventer
United Provinces of the Free Netherlands
Thursday, August 9, 1635

Dear Drika,
It is official. You are now an aunt. Luck was with me and the birth was not too difficult. Rener and I had the little one baptized on Tuesday. Her name is Francine. Francine Descartes, a fine name. What luck you and I have to live in the United Provinces, where the laws make sense. If Francine had been born in France, where Rener comes from, she would not be legitimate, merely because her parents are not married. Also, Rener says in his native country a mother does not give her newborn the breast. Instead the family hires a wetnurse. What a cold custom. Those French don't seem to understand too much. So why do they think they are smarter than us Dutch? But Rener is not like that. Every day he thanks me for my work. (I am still employed as a servant in the lodgings where he boards.) He talks to me about his writings, for he says I have a natural intelligence. We are so lucky, you and I, that our father taught us to read and write.

Rener says he and I will have equal say about Francine's future. But already he speaks of having her educated in Paris. In France she will learn more, he says. I am not so certain. What do you think? As you are my older, wiser sister, I would much value your opinion.

All my love
Helena

To René Descartes from Helena Jans

Santpoort
United Provinces
Saturday, September 1, 1640

Dearest Rener,
Please, you must return home at once. Our Francine has taken ill. At first she was only tired and I thought it was not serious. Then her throat got sore. Spots came up on her chest and neck. Now the rash reaches everywhere, even into her armpits. Her whole small body is an angry red, save around her mouth, where her skin has turned ghostly white. What worries me most is the fierce fever that refuses to leave her. I have brought in a physician and like me, he is mainly concerned about the fever. I had heard that bloodletting from the vein above the thumb can be good against fevers but the doctor has counselled me against all bloodletting from any part of her body. He says it may actually increase the fever. She is not to eat any animal food nor take cordials. He will not purge Francine, although he says when she has fewer symptoms he may treat her with a mild laxative. He says these are modern ideas of the English doctor Sydenham and he follows Sydenham's teachings in his own practice with some success. It is a way to achieve natural healing, he says. But I am not sure. How she suffers.

I waited a day to send word to you. Maybe this was a mistake, but I knew your meeting with your publisher in Leiden was important. In any case, I can wait no more. Come now.

I fear for our child. How can a little five-year-old defeat so big a sickness? Today, I began to feel unwell too. How will I care for our daughter if the disease strikes me?
Praying for your speedy return,
Helena

TO MARIA THERESIA HAGENAUER
FROM ANNA MARIA MOZART

Munich
October 12, 1777

Dearest Maria Theresia,

I send you fondest greetings from Munich where Wolfgang and I are on the first leg of our trip. Our purpose is to make as many introductions as possible and find for him—at last—secure employment. Why it has eluded him I do not know. Because he is Leopold Mozart's son, perhaps? Leopold dare not leave Salzburg now or he is sure to lose his assistant concertmaster position in Archbishop Colleredo's orchestra for good, and this so soon after his reinstatement. He had already lost the job once before, through missteps. Like father, like son? I hope not, at least in that respect, but considering Wolfgang's impetuous nature, who can say? What a terrible time I had giving birth to him and how that boy sometimes tests me still.

My apologies for not calling upon you prior to our departure on the 23rd of September. It does vex me that I failed to visit you, my friend of thirty years. How Leopold and I loved that tiny apartment we rented from you and Johann on Tanzmeisterhaus, where all our children were born—Nannerl, the five we lost, and finally our complicated little gift, Wolfgang. However brilliantly he plays and composes, Wolfgang worries me constantly, and not only because he is impossibly impulsive. He is also exceedingly innocent. Have we sheltered him too much, that he is so naïve about the ways of the world? I have seen much more of that side of him lately in our visits with Josef Myslevecek.

You may remember our speaking of Josef Myslevecek, the Bohemian-born composer Wolfgang and Leopold met in

Bologna seven years ago, when they stayed at the same inn. He has been such a champion of Wolfgang, talking about him everywhere, and trying to secure engagements for him, and Wolfgang says he has learned much about writing opera and string quintets from his older friend. Now Myslevecek is in hospital here in Munich receiving treatment for an unnamed illness. Leopold had heard that Myslevecek was disfigured, and suspecting a vile sickness, advised Wolfgang not to visit, but Wolfgang did anyway, and was much upset by his friend's unfortunate condition. Yesterday, planning a second visit to his ill friend, Wolfgang asked if I would come along, and I was happy to do so.

What a pleasant man and how we talked, Myslevecek and I, as though we had known each other forever. I could see, despite the hideous deformation of his nose, upon which surgery had been performed, that he had been, in better times, a handsome man. Apart from their musical affinity I can understand why he and Wolfgang get along so well, for even in his weakened state he is animated and delightful to speak to. He told me how he missed his identical twin brother, Jachym, who had taken up the family business of milling (something Josef himself had also learned to do, reaching the status of master miller) and was still living near Prague. The brothers had always been close; they had even attended Charles–Ferdinand University and studied philosophy together. But in the end, Josef's passion for music won out. He simply had to go off to compose. That is what prompted his move to Italy, where he has been living for the past eleven years or so. Still, he told me, he thinks of his brother every day. I told him how much I could feel his longing, as I was so close to my sister Maria Rosina, who was just a year older than I. We lived in the quiet village of St. Gilgen, and played together constantly. We endured the death of our father together, when she was five and I four, and she and my mother and I were obliged to move to Salzburg, such a confusingly large place compared to our small place of origin. We did not have much to spare, with my mother having only a tiny pension to support us, and Maria Rosina and I stuck together through everything, as closely as identical twins.

When I was eight, I lost my beautiful sister, and now at fifty-seven, I still miss her. All this I told Myslevecek.

He said, "Ah, how well you understand," and he took my hand, and he and Wolfgang and I sat in silence for a few moments. Later Wolfgang told me he had been thinking of Nannerl in those moments, missing his sister fiercely.

Myslevecek said he had taken a fall from a carriage and fallen on his nose, hence requiring the surgery. I believe he was sparing innocent Wolfgang's feelings; I recognized it was syphilis and thought no worse of Myslevecek for it. He made no secret of his freedom-loving life. He has always worked on commissions, never for an employer. And it is no secret that he has lived a free life in love as well, for which now, regrettably, he suffers.

From here we plan to travel briefly to Augsburg, and then it will be on to Mannheim, where Wolfgang hopes to convince the Elector to hire him as a musician in his court. Otherwise, we will go on to Paris, where we have many contacts, and seek opportunities for Wolfgang there.

It is quite the life, travelling around like this with Wolfgang—so different from the quiet of Salzburg. I love the excitement. Yet, I wish our family would travel all together now as we did when Nannerl and Wolfgang were children and we toured Europe showing them both off. It still bothers me that as they got older, Nannerl and I were left at home while Leopold took Wolfgang all over creation. Three trips to Italy and Nannerl and I did not get to go even once! Oh, how she pleaded with her father but you know how stubborn Leopold can be...there was no swaying him.

Farewell, for now. I embrace you as a sister and remain your devoted friend,
Anna Maria Mozart

To his mother from General James Wolfe

The paths of glory lead but to the grave.
—Thomas Gray, "Elegy Written in a Country Churchyard"

Banks of the St. Lawrence, 31 August, 1759

Dear Madam,—

Mr. Pitt chose the right man for this mission. Although he dislikes me and has said he suspects me to be a madman, he knows that once set upon a purpose, I do not relent. We *will* have Quebec.

Regrettably, for me personally, it is almost over. If the French and Canadian vermin do not kill me, I shall soon succumb to one of my ailments. Sad attack of dysentery in July, and you know about my fight with scurvy, which left me victorious but weakened. Rheumatism continues to torment me. But what will most likely take me down is the gravel, which has worsened. When it attacks, I pass a stone and the pain makes me cry out for instant death. If not the gravel, then the consumption or intermittent fever may end my life. In a way I shall be glad of the release. No strike by an enemy can create greater suffering than the body's assault upon itself.

I have asked the surgeons to patch me up well enough to see this campaign to its conclusion. So long as they do their duty, I shall do mine.

Our plans have been laid, in a general sense. I have acquiesced to the new strategy proposed by my three brigadiers, although two of them are villains and the third, an idiot. We shall devise a way to force the Marquis and his men away from their position and into the open, where we shall destroy them. They are greater in number but possess neither the training nor the experience of our battalions. The only fair weather month in this wasteland is October. It was heavy rain that thwarted our last attack in July. This time we shall not fail.

The proximate reason for this letter, however, is to guard against malicious conversation about me after I die and to request that you carry out certain of my wishes. As you well know, I have long predicted an early death for myself and have speculated that I would be required to give my life for my country. At thirty-two, I have already been granted double the time poor Ned had. To think that my brother died in Flanders—and had enlisted only to be close to me—causes me more anguish than any physical ailment can inflict.

Since you are my staunchest defender, I rely on you to ensure that society does not, in the coming days and years, labour under certain misapprehensions about me.

As regards the battle of Culloden thirteen years ago, a rumour has taken hold. It is said that the Duke of Cumberland asked me to finish off a wounded Scot who was ridiculing us, and that I refused, telling his lordship that he could remove my commission if he wished, but that I would not act as an executioner. The entire incident is a fabrication. Cumberland would never conduct himself in so dishonourable a manner or put me in such a position.

Moreover, it has been said that I remarked, on a recent occasion, that I would rather have written Thomas Gray's "Elegy Written in a Country Courtyard" than win Quebec. That is a lie. I am a soldier by profession, not a poet, much as I admire well-crafted verse. People hear that I have visited the court of Louis XV, and have studied Latin and mathematics, and perhaps they speculate that I would rather have had a more sedentary career. Never. We Wolfes are soldiers—my father, grandfather, uncle, brother, and I. It is true that were I to survive and return home, I would, of necessity, seek occupation more suited to an ailing person. Regrettably, however, I shall never again set foot in England. When I have gone to meet God, let no idle speculation interfere with the accurate public perception that I was, throughout my life, a military man by choice.

In recent days, some have unjustly represented me as ruthless. A military campaign is not a pretty thing; if a few farm buildings burn and animals lose their lives, it is not because we desire to quash the civilian population. It must simply be clear at all points that ours is the superior force. I have made it known here, by my own hand and in the French language, that Britain shows benevolence to the vanquished, so long as they do not rise up against us. It is in their interests to surrender; only French arrogance stops them from doing so. The intendant of their rough colony, Bigot, lives like an anointed monarch while the plain people struggle, and he encourages gambling in Quebec until it has become another disease. The dissatisfaction of the citizenry should be directed not toward me, but toward their own leadership.

This next part is for your eyes alone, lying, as it does, strictly in the private domain. Although you have not masked your displeasure at my engagement to Katherine Lowther, kindly see to it that she has her miniature portrait back, along with the copy of Mr. Gray's great poem that she gifted me when we were betrothed last Christmas. That you fulfill the moral duty to return these small items to Miss Lowther, I have specified in my will. However, I think it prudent to inform you now of my wishes in this regard. If you are tempted to forget to return those items to Miss Lowther, I would invite you to recall the pressure you exerted to have me end my courtship of Elizabeth Lawson, all because, as in Miss Lowther's case, the dowry offered was modest. It is only because of filial devotion that I die a bachelor.

Nonetheless, in every other respect, you have been always my champion and my comfort, and for those gifts I am grateful. Perhaps when you read these words, you will already be a mother with no surviving children. It saddens me to think of your grief. I am also sorry to leave you so soon after Father's death.

I wish you much health, and am, dear Madam,
your dutiful and affectionate son,
Jam. Wolfe

To Hermann Einstein
from Heinrich Schmidt

Luitpold Gymnasium
Munich
22 May 1892

Sehr geehrter Herr Einstein,
I write with great reluctance, since every parent wishes to hear
his son well spoken of by the boy's educators. This I cannot do.

Your son Albert neither fails nor excels in my Latin class. He
passes his examinations; however, his indifference to the subject
matter troubles me. He cares not whether we are studying
Caesar's *Gallic Wars* or Virgil's *Aeneid*; it makes no difference to
him whether I am teaching the rules of scansion or the uses of the
ablative absolute. Always he sits with a faraway look, as though
he were contemplating things not of this world. That expression
is most disconcerting to me as a teacher. I expect complete con-
centration from my students, who must not only be attentive but
also look attentive. As far as his participation goes, it is a repeating
story. "Einstein!" I say sharply, and I present him with a question.
He rises slowly, more like an eighty-year-old man than a thir-
teen-year-old boy. He hesitates, as though disturbed from some
more important occupation. Only then, and stumblingly, does he
answer. The fact that his response is correct is not the point. The
problem is his manner.

Once, he looked genuinely engaged in the lesson. The students were involved in silent work; they were translating Sallust's
Conspiracy of Catiline. Your son's eyes sparkled. I walked the aisles
of the classroom and soon discovered the reason.

Einstein was involved in a conspiracy, to be sure—not the
Catilinarian conspiracy, but a conspiracy of another kind,

between him and the contents of a geometry book, which he had embedded within the pages of the Sallust. Naturally, I confiscated the text and returned it only after Einstein had apologized to me in front of all my other students. His apology was flat in tone; it did not carry the ring of sincerity. I considered giving him a *Verweis*, but frankly, I did not think even a formal reprimand would cause him to experience, and, more importantly, demonstrate, penitence.

During the week I held that geometry book, I showed it to my colleagues in our Mathematics department and learned that the book is not even part of our curriculum. Later I discovered that your son has been caught in similar fashion twice in his Greek class. Once he was reading Kant's *Critique of Pure Reason*; the other time, he was poring over a work about light by a physicist named Tyndall. Again, not only not Greek, but also, not part of our curriculum.

If his inattentiveness does not end, I cannot say how or even if your son will make his way to the end of his studies here and indeed, one wonders how he will fare as an adult. I have never heard of an employer who will retain an absent-minded employee.

I understand this news is all harsh for you to hear but truly, I feel an obligation to inform you that your son needs to change his ways. He reminds me of Hoffmann's *Hans Guck-in-die-Luft*, the boy whose head is always in the clouds and winds up falling in the river, losing his notebook and facing deserved ridicule.

Do not let your Albert fall into the river, Herr Einstein. Through whatever means you have at your disposal, bring the boy back to earth, so he looks at what is in front of him—his Latin books, for example. Otherwise, his attitude will surely defeat him and he will not amount to much.

Finally, let me ask for your specific assistance with regard to his contraband reading materials. If you are able to ascertain where he is getting these items, kindly cut off his supply at the source. I thank you in advance.

With best regards,
Heinrich Schmidt

ANY WORDS YOU MAY HAVE FOR ME

Problem.
You cogitate. Cerebrate. Reflect.
Aha!
But wait. What if...?
You ruminate. You pace.
Face it: you need advice.
Now, articulate.

To Aphra Behn from Jane Barker

Christchurch Newgate Street, London
21 March, 1686

Dear Mrs. Behn,
We are not acquainted with each other, yet I beg you still to take
some moments to peruse this correspondence, for I have a critical
decision to make and would much value your counsel. You have
all my respect for your god-given capability to make words do your
will, and I have admiration for your labouring on notwithstanding
venomous statements related to your writings and slanderous comments related to your person. I am cognizant too of your perilous
travails as a spy for our country and have heard how harshly you
were treated for your pains, having received virtually none of the
remuneration promised to you, in spite of your regular entreaties.
In a world far more just than the one we inhabit, Arlington, who
defaulted utterly in his duty to pay you, would have faced the
rigours of prison to which you, instead, were subjected for failure,
through no fault of your own, to meet your financial obligations.
Moreover, I applaud your refusal to be deterred by the ravings of
those men who do not accept that women can write, and write
well. If the naysayers were correct, how to account for your published books and your many plays, produced on the great stages of
London and at the court of King James.

Now I must decide whether to avail myself of an offer and
it is my hope that, with your worldly wisdom and your experience in the publishing arena, you may see fit to advise me. I beg
your indulgence as I put forward here something of my own history and aspirations.

Stories and verses have been forming in my mind for as long
as I am able to remember; I recounted them aloud, as a small girl,

to my brother Edward, two years my elder and always a willing lis-
tener. Later he taught me to read and write and I set my childish
compositions down on paper, until little by little I came to write
more fluently, benefitting greatly from my brother's lessons in syn-
tax. As a young man my brother studied to be a physician at
Oxford and at my behest, when he was home for holidays, he
instructed me in anatomy, medicine and chemistry. Later I used my
knowledge to invent a plaster effective for the treatment of gout.

Although my choice is most unusual for a woman, I am
determined to write as my principal labour for however many
years God chooses to grant me life, craggy and fraught with perils
though the path to recognition may be. At present I find myself
low in spirits, with the pain of lone effort and omnipresent doubt
regarding my own aptitude, but as I have learned since taking to
the pen in childhood, such feelings advance and recede; beset as
I may be with apprehensions, I will not allow them to interfere
with my resolution to continue writing.

Six months ago my mother and I moved here from
Lincolnshire, but how long our sojourn in London will be, we
have not decided. It has become my custom to visit a bookshop
that lies at the western extremity of St. Paul's Churchyard, close
by where we are staying on Newgate Street. The bookseller,
Benjamin Crayle, I imagine from his appearance to be my age
(thirty-three) or perhaps a little younger, and I derive great pleasure in conversing with him, for, like you, I enjoy the company
of clever men. Mr. Crayle composes verses, although he has told
me he is not as serious a writer as I. From time to time, he pub-
lishes his own work as well as that of others. In an unexpected
gesture of generosity, or perhaps manipulation, he offered to
carry my gout plaster in his bookshop and to place, on the back
cover of a book of his verses, a notice regarding "Dr. Barker's"
plaster, its attributes and its availability at Mr. Crayle's bookshop.
As a result, I have made a little money from sales of the plaster,
but in spite of my repeated requests that he do so, Mr. Crayle
refuses to take any portion of the proceeds of sale.

Now, having read my verses, Mr. Crayle has offered to publish
a book of them. He assures me—for I have asked outright—that the

offer is made on the basis of the merit of the verses and is in no wise attributable to our camaraderie. Indeed, he states unequivocally that as a man of letters and in particular as a man of business, he would never consider publishing the work of an inferior poet. Because I do not have a reputation as a writer, I do not believe my name alone would excite the interest of the book-buying public, and I therefore have inquired of my poet friends at Cambridge, each of whom has a following of loyal readers, whether they would consider contributing some of their own verses to the book. To a man and with relish, they have consented. Mr. Crayle has looked at their verses and approved. Accordingly we now have a manuscript, half of which consists of my poetry, with the other half being devoted to the verses of the Cambridge lads. For the title I have suggested *Poetical Recreations*, and to that too, Mr. Crayle has agreed.

Yet I find myself bedevilled with hesitation. Should I be more circumspect than to take the first offer of publication that is given? Would the more prudent course for me be to inquire of other publishers, who might have greater resources than Mr. Crayle and who might, therefore, be able to distribute the book more widely? As there is a personal connection of friendship between Mr. Crayle and me, will publication lead to my feeling beholden to him in any manner? Are the terms of his offer reasonable, compared to offers extended to other writers?

A further consideration that I have not until now mentioned is this. Although I intend never to have my freedom curtailed by marriage, I do have and for the foreseeable future will have means of support apart from any proceeds of sale of my writings. My beloved brother Edward died of a fever at the age of twenty-five; it is a loss over which I have wept and written much, and from which I do not think I will ever fully recover. As a consequence of his demise, I was named as a "life" on the ninety-nine year extension of a lease to my father by the Earl of Exeter. The leased property includes a manor house, arable lands, and a water meadow in Wilsthorpe, Lincolnshire. My father, Thomas, who died four and a half years ago, had trained me in the management of lands, and I am particularly familiar with the Wilsthorpe manor and environs, where our family had lived since the 'sixties when my father was granted the original lease. I am both fortunate and grateful to have Wilsthorpe to rely on, but that does not cause me to waver in my determination to write for a living.

So as I am sure you appreciate, I do not wish in any way to compromise or even to appear to do so. Do you think if I accept Mr. Crayle's offer to publish, my doing so might be misinterpreted as anything beyond an agreement to enter into a mutually advantageous business arrangement? Am I acting too precipitously? Any words you may have for me, I would most appreciate, for you have broken the ground for me and, it is my hope, other women writers to come.

I am, dear Madam, with great esteem, yours very faithfully,
Jane Barker

To Catherine Churiau of Biarritz, France from Esther Brandeau

Hôpital Général
Port de Québec
Nouvelle-France
le 20 novembre, 1738

Chère Madame Churiau,
I trust you are in fine health and of good cheer.

A nursing nun, Sister Agathe-Louise, has become my dear friend and has offered to assist me. I simply call her Sister now, and she is the only person here who addresses me by my first name. Without her my loneliness would be unbearable.

I speak and Sister writes. From time to time she helps me find the right words. She tells me this letter will be transported on the next ship to France. I do not know if Biarritz is one of the ship's ports of call but Sister says the God she and I both believe in will ensure my words reach you. I hope that is so because I am much in need of guidance. I cannot decide whether to convert or stay Jewish. The rest of my life depends on the choice I make. The authorities here will not wait forever; I see them losing patience. If I do not succumb they will deport me—a terrible prospect, as with all my heart, I wish to remain here. If I do become a Catholic, it will be against my true will, and I will never be at ease with myself. I am pulled in different directions until I feel I will tear apart.

Sister suggested I write my parents for advice. But they have other children to care for. Moreover, since I was a little girl I have heard whispers I am illégitime and only my father's child, not my mother's, which may explain her coldness to me. As you know, I was fifteen and on a voyage to Amsterdam to live with relatives when the shipwreck occurred that brought about my good fortune—to be rescued by a fellow sailor, to meet you, and to live as a guest in your home. I could probably have somehow found my way back to my father's house in Saint-Esprit, as I was still in southwestern France. But I decided not to go back then and I choose not to ask my family for advice now. My mother always judged me harshly for my restless temperament. Even on short acquaintance, I felt more accepted by you.

Do you remember my excitement when you and I sat by your hearth and I had my first taste of pork ever? What a feeling of freedom that gave me. Above all, I value freedom.

I am sorry to have departed after only two weeks. I should have bade you adieu but in truth, I did not know I would leave until I was gone. I simply followed an impulse to keep moving.

Indeed, for the past five years I have been in motion, employed for the most part on ships, dressed as a boy and with my breasts tightly bound. I have been known by aliases, picking names that appealed to me. Most recently I called myself Jacques la Fargue and served as a cabin boy on the Saint-Michel under le Capitaine de Salaberry. On that voyage, I had a deep change of heart. Weary of constantly uprooting myself, I decided I would settle once the ship reached its destination—Québec. After all, I am a woman of twenty now, ready to set down roots. Salaberry saw past my male disguise, so I disclosed my true name to him. He did not punish me. It was not like other times I have been found out and whipped or worse.

We arrived in Québec in late September. "Catholique?" I was asked when we disembarked. "Juive," I said. Why would I lie, when my identity was already known? But that was when the trouble began, because, by law, Jews are not allowed in any colony of France. Thus, I have been given my options: convert and settle here or be sent back to France. Since I have at present no status and they do not know what to do with me, they have, for now, put me in the hospital. That is how I met Sister. She was one of those assigned to teach me Catholicism. She does her job; however, she has also become my confidante. We speak of many things now, not just religion, and she lets me say to her

whatever I please. I know she will repeat nothing to the authorities. My freedom to be myself with Sister is all that keeps me
sane. To Sister, I am a full person. To the others who visit me, I
am a conundrum and an embarrassment.

Other nuns come to see me. The parish priest comes as well.
The sessions are tedious. Constantly they make me pray with
them. Over and over, they explain the sacraments. What I hate
most is how they try to soften me up with references to Judaism,
as they argue that Christianity is its natural successor. Last
Tuesday, one of the nuns, Sister Marie-Joseph said, "As a
Hebrew you know the meaning of a sacrificial lamb. So of
course, you can see why Jesus is called the lamb of God." Truly,
I cannot. In fact I despise the original lamb tale. Abraham's binding of Isaac was an act of cruelty by a father and I wish that story
were not part of the Jewish religion. "Why do you think the
disciples of Jesus called him a rabbi?" the parish priest asked me
yesterday. "Perhaps to increase his popularity," I said.

They say I will learn to have faith by observing rituals. How
many times have they asked me to repeat the Apostle's Creed?
How can I, when I do not believe in 'Jesus Christ, His only Son,
our Lord, who was conceived by the Holy Spirit, born of the
Virgin Mary' and the rest of it?

They force me to attend Mass. Why? For how can I ever in
my life reach the point that I take Holy Communion, as those
who surround me do? Do they truly believe they eat Christ's
body and drink his blood? It defies reason. "That is not the
point," Sister Marie-Joseph has told me. "The Eucharist is above
human reason."

I know behind my back they call me fickle and flighty. I
am not. It is one thing to enjoy eating pork. It is another to
convert.

Sister says if only I would open my heart to Jesus, I could
become a nun. It was in the convent that she received learning.
But I wish to receive education without taking the veil. The
Ursulines teach some of the girls in this colony to read and write.
Perhaps I could join a class. What has the alphabet to do with the
Catholic faith?

Sister also says if I become a religious, I will not need to worry about being carnally possessed. Although I love her, I do not share Sister's anxieties about men.

I have been here for two months. Intendant Hocquart himself has come to see me weekly, to try to talk me into converting. He does not speak of religion, only practicality. He is not an unpleasant gentleman. I asked him what an intendant does and he said it is similar to being the manager of a company, except it is a whole colony he must manage. He is a large, ox-like man who moves his body as little as possible and talks slowly. I can see he would prefer to have a smoothly-running colony with no problems. "Be reasonable, Mademoiselle," he said in one of our earlier talks. "We are not asking you to stand at the right hand of the Pope or found a religious order. It is a simple thing, conversion." Just today, he told me it has been over fifty years since the law was made expelling Jews from French colonies in the New World. "That law was decreed by le Roi-Soleil, the Sun King himself," he said. "It is a law that admits of no exceptions."

"No?" I said. "Then explain Martinique, in the Caribbean. A French holding." After all, I have spent the last few years at sea and every sailor knows there are Jews living in peace and prosperity on that island. Without converting. "I cannot explain Martinique," the intendant said.

What do you think I should do, Madame?

As you can see I do not wish to convert, nor can the nuns and the parish priest and the bureaucrats here convince me, much as they may try. Even Sister, whom I love, has not been able to change my mind. It is true I still eat pork. And I have broken other rabbinic laws I will not mention. Still, I am Jewish. What Catholics have never violated rules of their own faith? Yet when they transgress, they do not convert to Judaism; they go to Confession.

It has occurred to me to pretend to embrace Catholicism, but secretly go on being Jewish. When I was a child my father told me about 1492. It is a famous year among my people—the year of the Alhambra Decree, when Jews were expelled from Spain. Some kept their religion and escaped, like my own ancestors, who moved to France. Others stayed in Spain and converted. But the ones my father called the anusim—the forced, in Hebrew—stayed behind and pretended to be Catholic but secretly practiced Judaism. Perhaps I am related to some anusim. I have been able to dress as a boy, change my name, adapt as needed wherever I have found myself. And yet I cannot contemplate being a Jew only in secret. That does not match my need for freedom.

If you have words of advice for me, please may I hear them, for I do wish to make my life here in Québec, but as a Jew, and I am much vexed.

Please accept, Madame, my best regards,
Esther Brandeau

To Jesus from Aristides de Sousa Mendes

June 17, 1940
Bordeaux, France

Beloved Saviour,
I pray you will make your mind known to me soon. For three days I have kneeled by my bedside, in deep prayer, in turmoil, and in hope that you or the Heavenly Father will visit me, talk to me, give me a sign, so when I emerge from retreat the answer will be obvious. I cannot stay away from my duties indefinitely but neither can I emerge until I am clear in my own mind.

In the quest for clarity, today I add this letter to my prayers, O Heart of Love. Forgive me, as I am bound to repeat the anxieties I have filled your divine ear with over these last days and weeks.

I call them the shipwrecked. They have congregated by the thousands, many of them Jews. They gather all over the city and in front of my consulate. They come from farther north in France, from Poland, from Germany. Some say they have seen their family members abducted or murdered and are sure to be apprehended themselves, perhaps killed, if they are forced back. I believe their stories. Who would fabricate such tales? They tell me it is imperative, for their safety, that they escape the continent.

I desire with all my heart to help them. Dear Lord, I know Portugal is officially neutral in this war. Despite my long service in the diplomatic corps, I find it hard to grasp what we mean when we say we are neutral. We allow our longtime allies the British to set up bases in the Azores—in Lajes for the Royal Air Force, in Faial for the Royal Navy—but at the same time we sell our wolfram to Hitler's Reich. The Germans convert the wolfram to tungsten for use in the manufacture of arms. It is well-known that our prime minister, Salazar, insists on payment in gold. Is he aware of where this gold comes from? Does he ask? Meanwhile, Nazi spies buzz around Lisbon, as common as houseflies. My government knows this well and tolerates their presence. Perhaps when we say we are neutral, we mean we will do business with anyone, as long as it is to our advantage.

As Consulate General for Portugal stationed in Bordeaux, I am expected to comply with Circular 14. It is specific in its terms. I must ask for permission from Lisbon before I grant exit visas, and clearly Jews are not favoured. I ask for permission, I wait for it, permission does not come. I ask again, I wait, I am met with silence. I ask a third time, I am told to be patient. This stalling continues, no movement occurs and I am told neither yes nor no. Is this what it means to be neutral?

Meanwhile the shipwrecked languish.

What if I grant them visas without waiting? Then they can pass through the French-Spanish border, and follow a route through Spain to Portugal, as others were able to do before them, before Circular 14. From Lisbon they can leave Europe and put the insane conflict behind them. Spain is also nominally neutral—and in Portugal, although there is not much appetite to accept Jews who pass through, at least we do not kill them.

I can help these people.

But, my sweet Saviour, at what cost? If I give them visas I must act alone and in defiance of the Portuguese government, my employer. Salazar does not like to be disregarded or obstructed and especially he will not countenance disobedience. With dictatorial fury, he will rage and then he will act.

I may lose everything.

How are my Angelina and our twelve children to survive, if I am stripped of my position, as is sure to happen? Will I even be allowed to practice law again in my home country or will that be taken from me too? My family, so respected in Portugal for many generations—what will become of their good name? What about the future of my children? Not just their survival but their education, their prospects for future employment, the way they are viewed by society?

How do I best serve God, you my beloved Saviour, and my fellow human beings in this circumstance?

Is it not my duty to protect my family?

Dear Lord, the shipwrecked gather in hordes outside my door. They are many; they are weary and hungry. And they are frightened, with reason.

Some days ago I spoke with Rabbi Kruger, who serves as a spiritual leader for many refugees. A brilliant and kind man, with whom I have formed a friendship. I thought perhaps if I could not help all, I could at least help a few, and offered to grant visas to his family. "All the people here—they are all my family," he said. If I turn the others down, he will not accept my help for himself, his wife and their children.

Are they all *my* family as well?

As much as my own wife and children?

I will know when it is time to arise from prayer. In your wisdom, you will tell me. I must do this thing or not do it. There is no neutral.

Your devoted and loving servant,
Aristides de Sousa Mendes

To Leo from AJ

July 31, 2012

Dear Leo,

I'm so happy you are getting that international summer school experience at Ajou University and it's great that you've learned you love bulgogi and bibimbap—in fact, *all* Korean food. Still, I sure do miss you. And here is my comfort: I know that when you return, you will have stories galore for me.

For now, though, correspondence will have to do, and you have certainly been holding your end up with your emails. I know you would prefer that I email you back, or text you, or send messages over one social medium or another or another, and, as you are aware, I try those means of communication from time to time. But I do appreciate your indulging me as I turn, the majority of the time, to my preferred mode, the handwritten letter. I think better with pen in hand than with fingers on keyboard. We've discussed the matter enough times and I know you understand.

Today I feel the weight of particular information. How I hope it is false. The load is heavy and I am not sure how to manage it.

You see, for whatever reason, I have been thinking about mayors lately—the good, the bad, and the surreal—so as I contemplated the stellar performance of our own mayor during the floods in Calgary last summer, it struck me that I would like to read more about a mayor for whom I have always had enormous respect and affection: Charlotte Whitton of Ottawa. You may not even have heard of her; she was well before your time, a Canadian public figure in the 1950s and '60s and earlier. Even for me, her active years occurred when I was only a child. But I learned about her as I got older and never lost my admiration for Ms Whitton. I liked her quick wit, her independence of mind, her role-modelling for other women who sought to participate in male-dominated activities such as politics and even hockey. (She was a star player at Queen's University.) It was no small feat, I am sure, to become the first female mayor of a major Canadian city—twice. Quite a bit of what we now call affordable housing went up in Ottawa under Whitton's watch and she made significant advances in the advancement of the profession of social work. All this I have known for a long time.

But it has been many years since I last considered the life and work of Charlotte Whitton. Yesterday, I decided it I wanted to brush up on my knowledge and discover whether someone had, perhaps, written a new book about this remarkable woman. If so, I was sure it would rightly be full of praise for her achievements. The weather was poor and I did not want to venture out to the public library. As a result, I did a search on the Internet (or the Intertube, as you call it when you tease me about my virtual cluelessness regarding technology). It is, in a way, a cruel medium. One sometimes discovers things too fast.

Now, Leo, you know I am neither naïve nor unthinking; I am not inclined to believe something is necessarily true merely because it has been written down. But after my Intertube search, I see documentation to the effect that Charlotte Whitton was antisemitic. It sounds as if she was not too fond of Ukrainians either. I am stunned. I knew she was in some ways a social conservative, but—a bigot? Or was she simply a person of her time?

How far her prejudices translated into behaviour I do not know. There is a difference of opinion on that. She sat on a committee in the late 1930s and, by some accounts, she strongly campaigned against a proposal to let orphans from Europe immigrate to Canada. Most of those children were Jews. So the children were returned to Europe and at least some wound up dead at the hands of the Nazis.

Did she know that would happen? I think it highly unlikely.

But what reasons did she give for opposing their entry? Well, it seems she was worried about the economy and had a go-slow attitude to immigration in general. I suppose that fits with her social conservatism. But still... to speak against the admission of orphans? A good part of her social work career was spent dealing with child welfare policies too. I can't make sense of her wanting to keep those children out of the country. The only explanation seems unthinkable: racism.

At the same time, I wonder if I am being fair to Charlotte Whitton. She is not here to speak for herself.

I am searching inside myself for a way to reconcile what I knew before with what I read yesterday. But I can't. As a result, I am heartbroken.

What do you think, Leo? You millenials understand, perhaps better than any previous generation, the importance of living with an open mind and heart. Maybe you can help me come to terms with what I have learned and how I now feel about a person who used to be one of my heroes.

Your friend,
Ariadne

To Golda Meir, Prime Minister of Israel
from AJ

Calgary, Alberta
Canada
May 3, 1972

Dear Prime Minister Meir,
Before I go further, I would like to wish you many happy returns on the occasion of your birthday. According to the Encyclopedia Britannica in the library here at Agnes Macphail High, you were born in Kiev exactly 74 years ago today.

Wholly occupied and preoccupied as you must be with affairs of state, I am sure you have little time to dedicate to correspondence that is not from a high-level source. Here I am, a simple fifteen-year-old Canadian girl. Yet, I prevail upon you to read this letter in its entirety and, if you would do me the honour, answer it personally, rather than passing it on to an assistant. (If the first reader is indeed an aide to the Prime Minister, please pass this letter on to your boss, and stop reading now.)

You see, Prime Minister, although I do not have, at this point, any particular political affiliation, I do have a strong interest in history, including history-in-the-making, and in people who are high achievers. I have followed your career from afar for the past five years, through international stories in our local newspapers, radio and television news, and Time Magazine, to which my parents subscribe. And I am currently faced with a puzzle that, of all the world's humans, *you* are the best equipped to help me solve.

Inspired in part by your own known excellence in debate, I approached my school principal, Miss Bochner, and asked if I might organize a debating club. She said that would be fine, as long as I could find a staff advisor and leave the classroom assigned to club activities in pristine condition after every use. I would also be responsible for making sure all chairs were placed upside down on their corresponding desks before my departure. Those conditions struck me as reasonable. I approached Mr. Peters, my Latin teacher, who occasionally reminisces in class about his days as a university debater. He enthusiastically consented to act as staff advisor.

My idea must have struck a chord because, with no more advertising than a mention in the morning announcements, we found ourselves with 27 members. In a democratically held election, they chose me as president. On the advice of Mr. Peters we set up an executive committee. And that is what I am so anxious for your advice about.

Our vice-president, whom I will call X, does not think I should be in charge because I do not, in his opinion, have enough education to do a sufficiently sophisticated job. Therefore, he feels it would be appropriate for me to voluntarily hand over the reins to him. True, he is in Grade 12 and I am in Grade 10. However (and I say this with as much objectivity as I can muster), he has an inflated sense of his own virtues and is driven solely by the prospect of being top dog. Meanwhile, our treasurer, whom I will call Y, does not want me in office because, he says in the vaguest of terms, I am "unqualified." In reality, it kills him to see me as president because I am a girl. It would be different if the club were girls-only, he says. Why do I not go off and organize an all-female club, he suggests; I am in over my head, he says. Our secretary, Z, is another story altogether. Monday, he declares his loyalty to me; Tuesday, he mumbles support for X's view that I am too ignorant to lead; Wednesday, he wonders out loud whether a female should be at the head of a mixed male-female group. Where his mind and heart will take him on Thursday is anybody's guess.

Of course, X and Y and, in his own inept way, the chameleon Z, chat all the time among the general membership, so what do we wind up with? Factions.

Now, as I have said, I have followed your comings and goings in Israeli politics as well as I can from so far away. And I know that four years ago you reached out to the Rafi, Ahdut and Mapam parties, which had all broken away from your own party, Mapai. You dealt with such big egos—like Moshe Dayan, the sabre-rattling swaggerer of Rafi, concerned mainly with power and control. How did you convince him to be on the same team as, say, Yigal Allon, promoter of a just division of land and a lasting peace between Israelis and Palestinians? And then there was Shem-Tov from Mapam, a party some people thought was too cozy with the Soviets. What a ragtag bunch they were, all at odds with one another. Hard to accomplish anything in such an environment, I am sure. And yet you managed to bring those people together, back into the Mapai fold, to form Israel's Labour Party. How on earth did you do that?

You see where I am going with this, Prime Minister. How do I bring my executive together? How do I reinstate esprit de corps in my club, now suffering grievously from disunity and unhealthy, ever-fluctuating sub-alliances? How do I act to make us strong, so we can put our energy into the work of becoming better debaters, not petty squabblers?

Please can you share with me how you got through to those stubborn people you had to deal with four years ago. Did you appeal to their higher natures? Cajole them? Reason with them? Make them feel guilty?

What I am looking for here is an effective approach. My domain is much smaller than yours (although Israel is not exactly big, as countries go). Still, like you, I wear the mantle of leadership and must take measures to restore my club to robust group health.

Yours in great admiration,
Ariadne Jensen

To Derek Wragge Morley from AJ

Calgary, Alberta
Canada
July 12, 1968

Dear Mr. Wragge Morley,

Allow me to introduce myself as a fellow ant lover. My parents gave me your fascinating book *The Ant World* for my eleventh birthday last month. I read it in one weekend, stopping only to eat and sleep. According to the back cover, you published your first research at the age of fourteen. So I know you will take me seriously.

I have a worry, it has to do with ants, and who knows more than you do about ants? My mother says I can mail this letter care of your publisher, Penguin Books Ltd., in Harmondsworth, Middlesex, and they will forward it to your home in Cambridge. That is what I am counting on.

Here, then, is the worry. As much as you and I admire ants, that is how much my neighbour Geraldine, who is slightly younger than I, despises them. She conducts her vile activities on the sidewalk. In my city our ants are mostly *Formicinae*, as far as I can tell, and they do not do well when Geraldine is around. She will set a paper on fire, throw it on the ground, fling a living *F. fusca* into the flames. She will tear off an ant's legs one by one, then decapitate the dismembered creature. She will stamp the life out of ant after ant with the sole of her shoe. One ten-year-old girl can inflict sizeable damage in this corner of the ant world, perhaps not in numbers wiped out, but in the degree of cruelty exercised in the act of destruction.

I have tried to get her to stop, to no effect. After I finished reading your book, I had some knowledge to go with my admiration of ants. And I thought if I were to share some unusual or amusing ant facts with Geraldine, she would not have the heart to continue her massacres. I showed her a picture of *Pogonomyrmex barbatus* of the Myrmicini tribe and explained that its name means "the bearded beardy ant." Hilarious! Not to Geraldine. Well, then, perhaps information with a disgusting ring to it might do the trick. I told her about the critical role of mutual regurgitation in an ant colony. She remained unimpressed.

Yesterday I figured out a sure-fire way to make her care.

With your permission, I will reproduce, as faithfully as I can, the conversation we had after my moment of insight.

ME: Geraldine, guess what?

HER: What?

ME: Some ants are dairy farmers—just like your Aunt Florence in Leduc.

HER: Eh?

ME: It's true. The ant strokes an aphid gently with its feelers— that's how the milking is done—and then the aphid spritzes out this liquid like honeydew and the ant laps it up. The aphid is the ant's cow, see? And when the ant is done with that aphid, it moves on to milk the next aphid in its herd. What do you think of that?

GERALDINE: Nothing.

ME: I know, it's exciting. And there's more. The ant looks after the aphid's eggs until they hatch, just like your aunt helps her cows with their calving. Isn't that something?

In response, Geraldine raised her right foot and brought it down hard, crushing three ants simultaneously.

Many lives are being snuffed out every day by that girl. What can I say to put an end to her callous behaviour? Would she think twice before killing if she knew there were variable intelligence between individual ants? Would she become a pacifist if she became aware of how highly developed a sense of smell her victims possess?

Or do I need an altogether different approach?

I would appreciate any suggestions you may have on how to deal with this disturbing and perplexing situation.

And once again, thank you for a thoroughly enjoyable read.

Yours respectfully,
Ariadne Jensen

OCCUPIED AS YOU ARE

With humility, one man accepts the top job with a complex out-fit. He lacks access to critical facts on a file. Someone should fill him in.

Another man has been after a top job for years. He waits his whole life, almost. Meanwhile, he makes mischief. Someone should talk him down.

AJ

TO POPE FRANCIS FROM AJ

Calgary, Alberta
Canada
January 16, 2015

Your Holiness,
I know your day must be indescribably full, occupied as you are with practical duties and of course, prayer. I admire the measures you have taken in recent months to clean up the curia, and, like so many other people, I applaud your desire to end inequality all over the world. That is why I am requesting your aid today.

You see, Your Holiness, in Alberta, Canada, the gay youth who attend Catholic schools need your help. They cannot attend Gay-Straight Alliance clubs, because GSAs are not allowed to exist in Catholic schools; thus it has been decreed by the Catholic school boards here.

Bill 10, which will become law if it passes just one more reading in our legislature, would allow a student to request that a GSA be set up in his school. But the request can be refused and the Catholic school boards have already said all their schools will indeed refuse. Then the student can appeal to the Minister of Education and the Ministry will set up a GSA. But since the Catholic school will have said no to providing space, the GSA would have to be somewhere other than the school. That will not work. Where is the support of the GSA needed? In the school itself. And what does the exclusion from the school do to students who wish to be in the GSA? It stigmatizes them further. That is why Bill 10 in its present form must be stopped. Yet senior Roman Catholic clergy in Calgary and Edmonton have spoken in favour of Bill 10. Perhaps you could have a word with them.

Why would I, a middle-aged woman who is not a member of the Roman Catholic faith (or, at this point in my life, any faith) feel so strongly about this subject? Partly it is because, like you and many other people of good will, I try to speak out about injustice when I see it. But also, I know a young gay person who almost died because of lack of support when he was in high school. So the matter is also personal for me.

You see, my dear friend Leo, now in his early twenties, attended a Catholic high school. He felt alone and longed for someone to confide in about his sexuality. Unfortunately he made the wrong choice—his parents. Do you know what they did when he told them he was gay? They threw him out of the family home. There he was, an innocent, sixteen years old, having to couch-surf in the homes of classmates' families. Can you imagine how he felt? It took two months and the intervention of Social Services before the parents took him back. Even then, they let him stay at home, but gave him no emotional support whatsoever. I'll bet you can guess what happened next, Your Holiness. Poor Leo tried to take his own life. He made two attempts, one with a belt and one with pills.

Leo is fine now. He is one of the lucky ones. You know the grim statistics as well as I do. Twenty-five percent of gay youth are kicked out of home when they come out as gay to their parents. What is even more horrific, one-third of gay youth try suicide.

And as we know, the sad reality is that some of them succeed.

A GSA in his high school would have been a great comfort to Leo at that critical time in his life. He says so himself.

There are other Leos in Alberta, Your Holiness. Please be so kind as to state your support for the mandatory establishment of Gay-Straight Alliance Clubs in all schools here, including Catholic schools, upon a student's request. And if you would be kind enough to explain to Archbishop Smith and Bishop Henry the value of such clubs, that would be lovely as well.

Thank you for your ear. I wish you a happy and productive pontificate.

Yours most respectfully,

Ariadne Jensen

To Prince Charles from AJ

Calgary, Alberta
February 23, 2013

Your Royal Highness,
It has been some years since I last wrote to a member of your family. On the only previous occasion, I invited your mother to tea. Her Majesty was about to visit Canada to celebrate the one hundredth anniversary of Alberta's entry into Confederation and I thought she might enjoy some respite from the commotion. Her Private Secretary of the day, Sir Robert Fellowes (who, I understand, has since graduated to a lordship), communicated on your mother's behalf, beginning his letter with these words: "Her Majesty the Queen has commanded me to write you."

I did not take umbrage when Her Majesty, through the agency of Sir Robert, declined my invitation. She is a busy woman. In any case, to be entirely frank, tea is not my cup of tea. I am more of a coffee drinker. However, anything to accommodate Her Majesty.

Like your mother, you are always on the go, I know. Lest you entertain any notions to the contrary, let me assure you that I am not about to invite you to tea. I do, however, request a few minutes of your royal time to share my anxieties—anxieties that I do not believe unwarranted—about your current state of busyness.

With due deference, sir, I am obliged to say that, at this juncture, there appears to be a growing gap between your reach and your grasp. Perhaps I can help you gain sufficient self-knowledge to recognize your own problem.

Let me begin by discussing a matter you learned about many years ago at Trinity College, Cambridge. I speak of the entirely unwritten British constitution. As you know, that constitution includes conventions, one of which dictates that the sovereign must maintain a neutral political stance, since there is a vast difference between the Prime Minister as head of government and the monarch as head of state. If you will permit me to say so, the latter position is largely ceremonial and has no connection whatsoever to the running of the country.

Yet you, Your Royal Highness, have written at least thirty-six letters to cabinet ministers in the past three years on a wide range of subjects. Moreover, you have held private meetings with some of those ministers to chat about your pet public policy topics. With the greatest of respect, sir, do you deem it appropriate for the Prince of Wales to promote homeopathy as a treatment to be covered by the National Health Service? Does not the very consideration of such a possibility lie outside your bailiwick as a prince of the realm?

About your outspoken revulsion by modern architecture, let me simply say that one person's carbuncle may be another person's castle.

Is it true that you have seconded some of your staff to cabinet ministers' offices? Please tell me that is a vicious rumour.

Granted, you are not the king. I suspect that nobody is more acutely aware of that than you. One day, however—difficult as it may be for you to believe—your mother will, in fact, die. If you have, in the interim, sent letter upon letter to Ministers of the Crown and have held private meeting upon private meeting with them, who will believe that you, in your role as king, will maintain political neutrality? Surely after so long and frustrating a wait, you would not want your brief reign to get off on the wrong foot.

May I suggest then, that you make a decision sooner rather than later. Would you like, in the fullness of time, to become king? If so, kindly stop writing those letters and put an end to those private meetings.

If, however, you feel compelled to make known your views on everything, including public policy, then I would recommend you renounce your right to inherit the throne, move out of Clarence House, and run for Parliament.

Yours respectfully,
Ariadne Jensen

I CAN EXPLAIN

Why do we do it? To advance? To thwart someone else's progress? To cover up a past wrong? Or for the sheer buzz of pulling off a deceit?

What is the draw? Why do we lie?

To Dennis Nassau from AJ

Calgary Alberta
September 12, 1971

Dear Dennis,

Thank you for your last letter, which I got today. I've been lucky to have you as a pen pal. I don't know even one other girl who has received letters from a real live American sailor. But. There's a lot on my conscience. I'm embarrassed. Out of fairness to you, I need to come clean.

You know how I told you I found your name and FPO address on the bulletin board of a community hall while I was visiting my cousin in Long Beach, California? That's true. However, it's not true that camera-shyness stopped me from sending you my picture, as you have asked me to do. Here's the real reason: In all my recent pictures I look about fourteen. That's because I *am* fourteen, not twenty-one like I told you.

I don't work as an assistant buyer in a bridal shop, with a supervisor named Miss Sacobucci. I don't work anywhere. I'm a high school student just starting Grade 10, or as you like to call it in your country, the tenth grade. So it follows that I didn't visit New York last spring with Miss Sacobucci. Everything I told you about my so-called visit to New York I got out of the Encyclopedia Britannica and my imagination. The farthest east I've ever been is Winnipeg, a cool Canadian city nowhere near New York. In fact, it's north of North Dakota.

In Phys. Ed. last year I failed the gymnastics part of the course, because I am a klutz. I lost my balance while walking slowly across the balance beam and fell, breaking my ankle. In other words, I have never participated in competitive gymnastics, as I claimed in my third letter.

My back yard is not lush with alpine asters and trembling aspens. There is no back yard. My family lives in an inner-city apartment. And since I am speaking of family, this is a good time to tell you my two older brothers are not in the Canadian military or the Brazilian military or any other military. That is because they don't exist. I am an only child.

I'm afraid there's more. My name is not Philomena Alhambra. I once went to a movie theatre called the Alhambra. As for Philomena, it's my favourite name. I think it has a romantic ring to it. My real name is Ariadne Jensen. Much more meat-and-potatoes-sounding, I know.

I could go on, but what's the point? By now you can see that before today, I have never given you any true information. I'm sure you are wondering why all the lies. I'm not sure. And that, believe it or not, is the truth.

I'm sorry. I don't expect you to write me any more.

Fair winds and following seas,
Ariadne

To Julius Fairchild from Peg Woffington

Southampton Street
London
17 April 1742

Dear Sir,

I beg your indulgence as I provide an explanation, one that is perhaps past due, in connection with our last encounter a fortnight ago. Your failure to grace me with your presence both last Thursday and today can only be attributable to my silence regarding what occurred.

I can well understand your displeasure when you called on me at three o'clock on 5th April, in accordance with our usual Thursday custom, and found strewn about in my bedchamber sundry menswear, including a waistcoat, breeches, square-toed shoes with a diamond buckles, and ribbed cotton stockings. The unwelcome sight of those garments caused you to depart summarily—and, as your grim facial expression revealed, in anger—without speaking a further word to me.

It is true the clothes are not mine—but neither do they belong to a gentleman. In fact they are the property of the Theatre Royal, Drury Lane, where, as you know, I make my living as a player. Although I have the part of Sylvia in our current production, *The Recruiter*, we are already in rehearsals for another of Mr. Farquhar's plays, *The Constant Couple*, in which I will reprise my role as Sir Harry Wildair.

Rehearsals are, of course, held at the theatre, but I also do considerable practising at home on my own. To engage in proper preparation for a role, I dress as the character I will be playing. Whether other actors follow this custom I do not know, nor is it my place to inquire. I am not one of those actresses like Kitty

Clive who feels she must look beautiful on stage; I would as soon play the ugly crone as the comely ingenue. And indeed, I am as willing to take a so-called breeches part as to I am to play a member of my own sex. However, my performances, once the play begins its run, are all the better if I practise beforehand in full costume, in my own time and not just when rehearsing formally with other members of the cast. As it happens, I was so involved in practising my Wildair part in my bedchamber on the Thursday before last that I quite forgot about the passage of time. When you called, I changed my clothing in great haste but alas, had insufficient time to put the costume away. Thus arose the misunderstanding.

Our arrangement is most pleasing to me, sir. I hope I have now disabused you of any anxieties regarding the small incident. If you would be so kind as to call on me next Thursday, the 26th April, at the usual time, be assured I shall receive you warmly, and with none of my costumes in evidence.

Believe me at all times with sincerity and affection,
Margaret (Peg) Woffington

UNFINISHED

You saw the need, you made a pledge, you laboured on. To bury your mentor with honour. To give the world your scientific work. To save your loved one's theories from theft. You strove until time called Time. Who will carry on?
AJ

To the president of my alumni association from AJ

Calgary, Alberta
September 1, 2012

Dear Alumni Association President,
Since my university graduation thirty-two years ago I have received numerous letters, phone calls and emails requesting a donation to my alma mater and I have consistently declined.

Once, when approached on the phone, I asked a question, and told your representative that if I received a satisfactory answer, I would donate. A callback within two weeks was promised but never came. Consequently, my response to all subsequent requests for funds has been negative.

Yet your pursuit continues unabated. Yesterday, within half an hour your representatives called me twice. Frankly, I've had enough. What to do? If I took my story to the media, they would not likely pick it up. After all, what is my angle? I have none.

Still, something must be done.

So I have decided to appeal to your higher nature, and explain to you personally why my alma mater will never see any of my money. In return, please call off your alumni-siccing dogs.

Let us return to my university days. I was shy, and a keener. Between classes, I studied. The libraries were my favourite places to read, think and write.

The first time it happened I was at the main library, seated at a long table. I had tried and rejected the square four-desk units. When I sat there I felt hemmed in. (Also, the interlocking pattern of the wooden frame at each unit's top bore an unsettling resemblance to a swastika.) At a long table, I could see other students and the occasional professor come and go. Other people often sat at the table too. And although we did not interact, I found their presence comforting.

The stacks were to my left. I saw a student wandering through them. He'd pick up a book, return it to the shelf, take a few steps, pick up another book. He looked aimless. With his wire rimmed glasses, t-shirt and scraggly hair, he resembled many other boys on campus. But then I noticed he was wearing cutoffs and, well, his penis protruded from the bottom. I was frightened. I gasped, gathered up my books and sprinted to the circulation desk to report what I'd seen. "All right," the librarian said. Her tone and expression were flat. I may as well have told her I was returning an overdue book.

Later that day, ready for another study session, I chose the Physical Sciences library. Its design suited my preferences perfectly—long tables only. No cubicles. I enjoyed using the various science libraries, filled, as they were, with the geeks of my generation. (My fellow Arts students preferred the social over the academic.) I opened my American Literature Anthology and got to work.

As I sat reading "Sinners in the Hands of an Angry God," an early American writing by the hellfire-and-brimstone preacher Jonathan Edwards, who should walk through the turnstile but the exhibitionist in cutoffs. Clearly, the woman at the circulation desk in the main library had not called the police or even campus security after I spoke with her. When Mr. Cutoffs first arrived at Physical Sciences, no parts were exposed. He headed straight for the stacks. A few minutes later I saw him again, pulling the same trick as he had earlier in the day. Clearly, he had been emboldened by getting a reaction from me the first time and then facing no consequences from the authorities. This time I was clear-headed but angry. I walked to the circulation desk, gave my incident report and received the same blasé reaction as I had gotten at the main library. The two librarians could have been the same person, the only difference between them being hair colour.

A week later, on a chilly winter night, my classmate Alicia and I were leaving campus when we came across a different guy, about our age, standing in front of the student union building, exposing himself. Unlike me, Alicia was a quick thinker. "Put that thing away," she said. "You'll catch your death of cold." She found the incident amusing but I was shaken.

I became depressed from those sightings on campus and my lingering memories of them. The pressure of exams and papers got to me. I was lonely and disoriented, being so far away from my family and home town. Finally, I dragged myself to the university's health clinic where I filled out a questionnaire and was given an appointment with a psychiatrist.

"I think you're just a little blue," he said. "Go out and get drunk."

"But I'm barely eighteen and I don't drink," I said.

"Learn," he said.

Then a guy in my introductory anthropology section suffered from a break from reality in class, and trembled and screamed until he was taken away. He spent a year in treatment. The university kicked him out. Two years later they let him return but with strict conditions. He couldn't do this, couldn't do that. He was not allowed back on the university basketball team because... well, they never did say why.

Now I will share with you the question to which I never received an answer. What is the university doing to help students preserve their mental health, or restore it if they lose it?

Sincerely,
Ariadne Jensen

To her daughter Gabrielle-Pauline
from Emilie du Châtelet

le 2 septembre 1749
Lunéville
Duché de Lorraine
France

Ma chère Gabrielle-Pauline,
I must speed my pen along as my *accouchement* fast approaches.
From the start of this late pregnancy I have had premonitions of
dying in labour. While I put no stock in superstition, my fears are
far from irrational. At 43, I am much too old for birthing; all the
usual perils multiply. I fear my time is short. Thus has arisen my
resolve to raise with you now two matters we have not discussed
directly before: my reputation and your education.

You know the life of the court—how rumours proliferate,
how whispers fill the corridors. Place no credence in remarks you
may have already heard and are likely to hear all the more after
my death. Scandalmongers will hiss about your father and me,
Voltaire and me, the Marquis Saint-Lambert and me. Know this,
my beloved daughter: every man in my life whom I have loved,
I have loved fully, body and soul. Indeed, when they are behav-
ing at their best, those men show tolerance, even friendship,
toward one another.

With your father being so much older than I, he brought
maturity into our marriage. Always he has treated me with kindness. You know he has been away on military campaigns for
years at a time; what you may not know is that, from the first,
we have had a tacit understanding. As for Voltaire, he and I continue to be close friends and colleagues, although we have had no
physical intimacy for five years now.

How many noblewomen on this continent have taken lovers and not lost any standing? One can easily lose count. But for me, it has been different. My involvement in physics, mathematics and philosophy is what really bothers my detractors, women and men alike. My insistence on using my mind—that is what they hate. What I do with my body is merely their excuse. For devoting myself to study and research, I have been labelled a courtesan and worse. When I am gone and you hear the cries of condemnation, remember the truth of your mother.

Now we come to the matter of your education. If you would like for it to continue, I am sure that is accomplishable. Even as a little girl, you showed high intelligence. In my own childhood I was fortunate: at my request, and over my mother's objections, my father brought in tutors for me. Never before now have I shared with you how, when I was ten, the magnificent old astronomer Fontenelle graced our family's dinner table and taught me the wonders of the night sky. Why did I not offer such stimulation to you? Was it because you did not ask? Perhaps I was too absorbed in my own lessons—after our marriage, your father paid for my tutors, Maupertuis and Clairaut. Perhaps I did not take proper notice of your intellectual needs. Perhaps I should have been a tutor to you, sharing with you my own learning.

Now, I fear it is too late for me to help you learn. It is good that you are happy in the marriage to Alphonse that your father and I secured for you, and I am pleased that you enjoy serving as a lady-in-waiting to the Neapolitan queen. But, dear girl, if you find the duties of your station insufficient to bring you full satisfaction, and you wish to study, by all means tell Alphonse, and if he is not receptive to paying for your tutors, ask your father, who will gladly attend to their remuneration. Do not be dissuaded by those who wish to restrict the scope of your interests.

I must apologize now for some of the strictures placed upon you as you were growing up. How you wept when I sent you, as a seven-year-old full of life, to the Couvent de la Pitié! I did not intend that you stay sequestered forever; on the contrary, I hoped the good sisters would enrich your education. I listened to your pleas to come home the following year, but I cannot explain why I made you endure that convent life again when you turned eleven. It was a misjudgment on my part, one for which I hope you will forgive me. At least I did not keep you in for as long the second time. Now that you are a fully mature woman of twenty-three, your comprehension is more profound. Please realize I made all choices for your future, both the right ones and the misguided ones, with your well-being as my greatest consideration.

There is little left for me to do now but wait. I had such severe discomfort two days ago I thought I would be delivered of the child then, but the cramps stopped suddenly. Of course one never looks forward to the labour and birthing pains, the six weeks that feel like six months of lying-in, the milk fever, the binding of the breasts to arrest the flow. Still, how relieved I will be if I have the good fortune to survive. And despite the trial I must endure, I could not ask for a more beautiful place to undergo it. Stanislas, the Duke of Lorraine, has taken a liking to me. He read my book on Leibniz and enjoyed it. I could not with grace decline his offer of these bright quarters in Lunéville, where I can go through the entire process in relative privacy, yet with all the necessary medical and personal assistance.

The premonitions have been strong and I have taken heed. In addition to talking with you, I had another task to complete: my Newton. I spent some time in Paris recently and worked constantly, stopping only to eat and sleep. As a result I managed, two days ago, to finish the translation of Monsieur Newton's *Principia Mathematica* from the original Latin into French. I have added my own commentary as well, something I could not have done without the calculus Clairaut taught me. I have sent the manuscript to the director of the King's Library. Should I not survive, I know Voltaire will see to it that the work is published.

As I write, the pain in my back increases. Labour is close, or perhaps upon me already. I shall put this letter into the hands of Longchamp, Voltaire's servant, whom I trust even more than I do our du Châtelet family intendant de la Croix. I will instruct

Longchamp to hold the letter in confidence and send it to you in the event of my death.

I am, my dear, your most affectionate and devoted mother, Emilie du Châtelet

To Abate Jacopo Panzanini
from Vincenzo Viviani

Florence
April 5, 1702

Dear Jacopo,
This morning, as I mark in quiet fashion my eightieth birthday,
my mind naturally fluctuates between images of the past and
thoughts for the future. With no illusions of achieving immor-
tality, I write today to impress upon you once again the
importance I place on an unfinished project of mine. I am determined to see that my teacher Galileo is moved to the resting
place of his own choosing, where his memory will be honoured
with a fitting headstone. The responsibility for this undertaking
I took at the age of nineteen. I have made my best efforts over
these many intervening years, and indeed I continue to try, to
the extent my health permits; however, there have been constant political impediments to what should have been a simple
venture. In consequence, it will most likely fall upon you, my
nephew, my sole successor, to ensure that the undertaking is carried out. It is you who will oversee the project—to bring the
greatest scientist of the seventeenth century—perhaps of all
time—to the location he requested in his will—next to his own
father's remains in the Basilica of Santa Croce. As you shall see
when the time comes, my will sets out in detail what you will
need to do and how. I have left instructions on the construction
of a dignified monument, the cost of which will easily be met
by my estate. Because you are not only a man of the cloth but
also a mathematician in your own right, with an appreciation of
my teacher's genius, you will, I am confident, take your solemn
assignment to heart.

It does not seem so long ago that I arrived at Galileo's villa in Arcetri, where he had unjustly been placed under house arrest and was living out what remained of his time on earth. How fortunate I was, a sixteen-year-old, to have already studied geometry under the Galilean Clemente Settimi, who mentioned me to his own teacher Michelini, who in turn arranged for me to have an audience with the Grand Duke Ferdinando. It was the Grand Duke himself who recommended me to Galileo as his assistant. Why did that honour fall to me, not another? Perhaps because I was fortunate enough to have a great love of mathematics (in which, however, I felt I had little strength) and also the vigour of youth.

If only you could have been with us during those last three years of my teacher's life. Elderly, sick and blind, Galileo of course relied on me and others for practical help. However, he showed enormous vitality of intellect as he talked of science almost continuously, trusting me to write down all he said and inviting me to participate. Together we conducted many experiments to test theories.

If only Galileo and I had had the means, through experimentation, to unravel time and change his past. How I wish we could have eradicated the years my teacher was persecuted by regressive elements; if only we could have replaced them with years of free movement, acceptance by the church, and universal admiration. But we humans do not inhabit a land of dreams.

To ensure Galileo's body is moved and the monument erected, you must combine determination, close observation and diplomacy. Do not let my campaign of the past sixty-one years go to waste. Look for every opportunity to influence Grand Duke Cosimo. He seems always to be at prayer or in travel; I cannot make him understand the importance of Galileo, as his father Ferdinando did. Perhaps you can achieve what I could not. Moreover, should a Florentine occupy the papacy, petition him as soon as you can, for he would not want the body of my teacher to languish in obscurity. What you must do is get both religious and secular authority on your side, or at the very least convince the pope, who will then exert pressure on the duke.

I know we have spoken of this matter before. However, as the end of my own life draws ever nearer, I find the need to state the case once again as emphatically as I am able. I put my trust in you to comply with your duty to see Galileo to his proper resting place and I hope you will take pleasure in doing so.

Your devoted uncle,
Vincenzo Viviani

To Aspasia from Xanthippe

Athens
Hekatombion 18
Ol. 93, 4

Xanthippe to Aspasia, greetings.

I write you on a matter of some urgency, although nothing dire has yet come to pass. Nevertheless, I see Athens going downhill, our treasured democracy collapsing, and I fear for what may lie ahead.

Especially I worry for my husband, and what will become of his work when he is gone. Even if he lives out a full natural life, how much longer can it last? As you know, he is in his mid-sixties.

For as long as we have been together, I have been trying to convince Socrates to write his ideas down. He simply will not listen. I should not be surprised. This is a man who will not charge a fee for his work and refuses to buy a pair of shoes. If I cannot convince him in such basic matters, how can I talk him into something as important as recording his thoughts?

Socrates believes it is only through speaking with others that he can do his work. No writing, he says, can accurately represent the questions that lead to responses that lead to more questions. He would lose the threads of argument, he says, the nuances of tone, all the features of conversation that enhance meaning as he engages with people.

I think much too often about the twisted and ridiculous caricature of my husband in *The Clouds*. Aristophanes had not even met Socrates when he wrote that wretched play. Now they are good friends and Aristophanes has changed his mind. But the play stands. It has been produced and will be produced again, perhaps well beyond our lifetimes. And because the play has been written down, it will be read. Will its future audiences and readers think the real Socrates is the manipulative, greedy Socrates of *The Clouds*? How will they know the truth of my husband?

I worry, too, that some of the younger men who follow Socrates will wait until he dies, and then write down what they think he said, when he is not present to correct them. Xenophon and Plato are the two I suspect the most. They always have tablets and styluses with them when they walk with Socrates. What do they write down? Why does Socrates not ask to read their writings? Those two may have ideas of their own that they want to promote. What if, after Socrates dies, they attribute their own ideas to him, or they say he endorsed those ideas, in order to give themselves more credibility? Worse, what if Xenophon or Plato puts forward a theory as his own—but it is really Socrates's?

I worry about what they will write but also about what they will not write. Socrates opposes slavery. It is natural for him to feel that way, coming, as he does, from a modest background as the son of a stonecutter and a stonecutter himself until he took up the calling of philosophy full-time. Xenophon and Plato are aristocrats. Will they write down that Socrates believed slavery to be wrong? Or will they omit to mention that, because it is not convenient for them?

Socrates also believes women should receive the same education as men; that our lowly place in society should be elevated. I have always suspected Plato of having the heart of an oligarch. Will he write down that Socrates believed women should have equal rights?

The sycophant Alcibiades is another one I do not trust. He follows my husband around like a puppy, gazes at him with such admiration it is sickening to watch. I am certain by now he has offered his alluring young body in exchange for the opportunity to explore the depths of my husband's mind. Whether Socrates has accepted I do not know. I do not inquire into such matters. But if Alcibiades decides to record something about Socrates, what will it be? What will he write down?

I know my husband thinks highly of you, not only because you wrote speeches for your dear Pericles, but also because of your grace on the many occasions that philosophers have assembled at your home to exchange ideas.

Would you consider doing something for me? Would you walk around the city with Socrates every day for, say, thirty days, as he engages in his conversations? Afterwards, write down what he and his interlocutors have said. Then there will be at least one written record that is wholly accurate. That will set my mind at ease. I will have some copies made; in fact, I have just purchased a good quantity of papyrus for the purpose. We can discuss fee privately. Be assured that our acquaintanceship will not stand in the way of my paying you a fair price for your services.

I must admit to a much smaller, secondary purpose. By taking this action I hope to rehabilitate my own reputation. I am thought to be respectable, but a shrew. I am not sure where the misperception originates—certainly not with Socrates. If a few kind words about me were to find their way into the writings, I would be pleased.

Favour me by taking care of yourself and Young Pericles.
Fare well.

WORK WITH ME

To fulfill a mission of kindness. To execute a project of passion. The key, to collaborate.

AJ

To Joan of Arc from AJ

May 30, 2013

Dear Joan,

It is impossible to know if this letter will get to you. Personally, I am agnostic and have no idea whether there is any substance to the Christian promise of life after death for the deserving. Moreover, if there is a heaven, can it be reached by Canada Post? Another unknowable.

Still, I must make the attempt, as a friend of mine finds herself, from time to time, in serious psychological trouble and I think you may be in a position to assist. My friend's name is Joan Himmelfarber. We have known each other since childhood. My family had a television; hers did not. When we were seven years old, and she was over at my house to play, we watched a rerun of the show "You Are There," hosted by Walter Cronkite. It featured an interview with "you" as performed by an actress. The interview was conducted in a replica (supposedly) of your prison cell. My friend Joan was enchanted by your story. She read about you; she practically memorized *The Lark*, Anouilh's play about you. In her teens, Joan learned that you hardly ate. As a result, when adolescent social anxiety took its toll on her, she stopped eating much. Shunning food made her happy, she told me at the time, because it made her feel closer to you. Her parents were worried. They were afraid she was anorexic and took her for help but she would not listen to any of the doctors. Her menstrual periods stopped, as often happens when girls do not eat, and that only increased her euphoria because, as she explained to me, you did not menstruate either.

When we were at university, both members of the film society, Joan took me to see the 1928 silent movie *The Passion of Joan*

of Arc. We watched transfixed as Maria Falconetti, under the bru-
tal direction of Carl Dreyer, portrayed you as a terrified teenager
in your last days on earth. I knew, but was careful not to tell my
friend Joan, that Falconetti never appeared in another movie and
took her own life some years later. Still, after watching the film,
my friend's fascination with you only grew.

By the time Joan reached her twenties, her preoccupation
had taken a new twist. At times, when under stress, she would
suffer a temporary break from reality and, in her mind, become
you. It happened shortly before an operation for a broken leg following a fall from a balcony. (There was some question as to
whether it was actually a jump, in another of her attempts to imi-
tate you.) She interpreted her exam room at Emergency as a cell
and complained that her "jailers"—the nurses on the floor—were
trying to rape her.

Decades later—Joan and I are in our fifties now—the problem persists. Or perhaps it would be more accurate to say the
problem continues to resurface. Recently, in a job interview
conducted by three executives, including an intimidating human
resources professional, Joan felt intense pressure and morphed.
She answered business questions with talk of messages received
from Saint Michael, Saint Catherine, Saint Margaret. When the
human resources professional said "We'll let you know, " Joan
asked if she would have their answer before or after the crowning
of the Dauphin.

As far as I can see, Joan's lapses into Joan-of-Arcdom do not
affect her on a day-to-day basis. The delusions only overtake her
when she is under extreme stress. Who understands stress better
than you, after your experience with your inquisitors? What ter-
ror you must have felt when they showed you those instruments
of torture. No wonder you broke temporarily and recanted. Rest
assured we have all forgiven you that short-lived mistake. Stress
does funny things to people.

It may strike you as ironic that I would communicate in
writing with you, since in life you were illiterate. Well, it seems
to me that sometime in the past five hundred eighty-two years,
someone up there must have taught a bright young woman like

you to read. After all, illiteracy is a kind of hell and surely the powers that be in your eternal dwelling place would not leave you in such a state of suffering. You already burned once, in life. That is enough.

But to come back to my friend Joan Himmelfarber, I am sure you are by now eager to know how you can ease her burden. I do not think it should be too difficult. Would you mind simply making your presence known to her, in much the same way that Saints Catherine, Margaret and Michael made their presence known to you? She is sure to recognize your voice so I do not think you need bother with any visual representation. I know you speak French but I am sure something similar to Star Trek's universal translator can be employed to overcome the language barrier. Please inform my friend gently but firmly that there is only one Joan of Arc and you are it. I think she will listen to you.

Frankly, if you do not intervene, I fear for Joan's sanity. What if, on some future occasion, she morphs into her Joan-of-Arc persona and is unable to come back? If you can pre-empt such an episode, I would be grateful. I know you understand, as your own sanity was so often called into question once the English, their lackeys the Burgundians, and Cauchon's dirty inquisitors came after you.

Thank you for your anticipated assistance.

Sincerely yours,
Ariadne Jensen

To Joseph Pujol from Onésime Lavallé

Paris
le 27 mars 1908

Dear Monsieur Pujol,
Allow me to introduce myself as an admirer of both you and the art form you have mastered.

I found it enchanting to watch your cabaret in the '90s. Indeed, I returned three times and never wearied of your act. Such musicality! Originality! Panache!

I was appalled when you were dismissed merely for sharing your unusual gift from time to time outside the confines of that one establishment, the Moulin Rouge. Monsieur Zidler seems to have the impression there is something sacred about his cabaret. He had no moral right to keep you from your public, which is to be found everywhere, because of the universal appeal of your unique mode of performance.

My heart sang when you won your lawsuit, wherein you proved that the charlatan who succeeded you at the Moulin Rouge, styling herself "the female pétomane," was far from being *la vraie chose*. I was not at all surprised when it was revealed that she used a crude bellows hidden under her skirts to simulate the effects *you* produce naturally, *sans* external accoutrements or paraphernalia.

Last year, I found myself in Marseilles conducting several weeks of research for a historical novel when I learned, to my delight, that your travelling show, Le Théâtre Pompadour, was about to pass through the city. What an opportunity for me again to witness your genius at work! Your performance far exceeded my expectations. I was especially moved by the performance of Monsieur Debussy's recent composition "Clair de Lune," rendered by your wife on piano and accompanied by you on your natural instrument. Or perhaps it could more correctly be said it was she who accompanied you.

There is, as far as I can tell (and I have made a point of investigating the matter) no other living individual in Europe who has perfected farting as an art form. Moreover, I am astonished that you do your work odourlessly—something that cannot necessarily be said for the pétomanes mentioned in medieval writings.

As I believe I have already mentioned *en passant*, I am a writer by trade. Like many who share my calling, I have not yet experienced quite the success of Zola, de Maupassant and Dumas. Nevertheless, I have a vision for an artistic collaboration with you. The limelight will stay where it belongs—on you—while a modicum of attention may fall on my own modest talents.

I propose that we produce a piece of theatre, a dramatic history of your own electrifying life and ascent to fame. The show, a one-man production, to be called "Sharps and Flatulence," would be performed by you in words and farts. The words would be my contribution, delivered in your sonorous voice. My involvement would be strictly behind the scenes. Through rehearsal we would work out the proper points at which you would add retorts, imitations, explosions, musical renditions, and other such flourishes, using your special talent. To keep audiences returning, we would present the spectacle in instalments, in the fashion of the *romans-feuilletons* of Honoré de Balzac and Madame Sand. We know a fascinating story told in serial form can sell newspapers. Similarly, it can sell theatre tickets, especially when the story is told in such a novel manner.

Let me assure you, Monsieur, my interest in what you do predates even my acquaintance with you. As a boy I was privileged to have an English-language tutor, an American, who caught me making farting noises one day during a lesson. I expected punishment, but no…instead he taught me an English expression attributed to the first ambassador of the United States to France, Benjamin Franklin: "Fart proudly."

Although I now find myself in middle age, my interest in the potential of skilled farting has only increased. And in your practice, you have brought about the seemingly impossible—the conjunction of bodily function and high culture.

Should "Sharps and Flatulence" succeed artistically and critically, as I believe with all my heart it will, perhaps we can collaborate on further projects in future. Perhaps the shows can travel, even beyond the borders of France, so that your magnificent talent can be witnessed by audiences *hic et ubique terranum*—here and anywhere on earth.

I await your response with great anticipation and optimism.

Please accept, dear Monsieur, my most respectful salutations,
Onésime Lavallé

YOU NEED NOT REPAY IN QUARTERS

Cashier misreads you, waiter slights you, repairman dawdles, service provider leaves a confusing message.

Trivial occurrences?

Or symptoms of a civilization in decline?

AJ

To the owner of the Café Versailles from AJ

November 27, 2013

Dear Owner of the Café Versailles,
I am a regular patron of the Café Versailles and am, on the whole, happy with the service. My friend Leo often accompanies me. We like places where we can pay in advance at the counter, so the Versailles suits us perfectly that way. Last Wednesday, an incident occurred. Some would call it insignificant. Not to me. I cannot get the event out of my mind and I feel it warrants your attention.

The exact words used are critical. I remember all of them—for some reason, I have the ability to recall many conversations verbatim—and am therefore able to give you the following precise account of the verbal exchange between one of your staff and me:

"Excuse me… I didn't get enough change. I'm sure it was an accident, because you were busy. But I am five dollars short."

"Uh, I don't think so."

"I gave you a twenty. For two cups of tea—one Earl Grey, one green. "

"Yes."

"And you gave me this change. What I am showing you right now."

"Plus a five dollar bill."

"No, that is what you forgot."

"I did not."

"But I haven't even put the change away. As soon as I got to my table I saw the error. And I don't have a five in my wallet."

"Oh, I gave you the five. I sorta know I did."

"But I come here all the time. You've served me before."

"I know what I gave you."

"I would like to speak with the manager, please."

"Oh fine. Here's a five."

"Thank you. But I can see you still don't believe me."

"Sure I do. Sure I do."

As a successful entrepreneur, you are aware of the importance of tone in all commercial transactions. That is particularly the case in a business reliant on customer service, word-of-mouth referrals and return business. I was not happy with your staff member's tone or language, both of which clearly implied that I was a liar and a thief.

I am not asking you for anything. That is why I have not described the worker in question, nor even disclosed that person's gender. I would, however, suggest that you remind all your staff of your expectations in their dealings with clientele. Perhaps they need to learn about courtesy and giving the customer the benefit of the doubt.

May I also respectfully suggest that you make the occasional unannounced visit to the café. There may be more going on at the Versailles than you realize.

Sincerely,
Ariadne Jensen

To the owner of Flowmayvin Trenchless Sewer Repair Ltd. from AJ

October 23, 2012

Dear Sir:

I am writing on a matter that may seem, at first blush, insignificant to your business. What, after all, do the wording, punctuation and format of a note have to do with the maintenance of sewers? Until twenty-four hours ago, I would have said there is no connection at all, which is likely your view too. By the time you have read my letter, though, I believe you will agree the links are strong.

Yesterday I found a note from your company suspended from the bottom of my apartment mailbox. Identical notes awaited the other occupants of the apartment building. As a person on top of your business in both senses, you know precisely what that note said: *The trenchless sanitary pipe rehabilitation scheduled on your block today, has been cancelled.*

I was puzzled. When you wrote "cancelled," did you mean cancelled for all time? Or did you mean deferred to a later date? I have seen the word "cancelled" used both ways in recent years. You can understand how the ambiguity might trouble the other building occupants and me. If the cancellation were permanent, we would consider our sewer worries over for the foreseeable future. If, however, the work needed to be rescheduled, when would it be done? And where would that leave us in the interim? We do not have your expertise in trenchless sanitary pipe rehabilitation. (Indeed, it takes a certain kind of personality to conduct rehabilitation of any kind, and neither I nor my co-occupants in the building, from what I know of them, are cut out to work in the rehab field.) We rely entirely upon you when it comes to the health of our sewers, and now we do not know what to expect.

I was also taken aback by the presence of the comma after the word "today." I wondered what that comma could mean. Clearly, the note was in a standard printed format, intended to be sent to different people on different days as circumstances dictated. My first idea was that you had intended to insert the date of the relevant "today" to suit each situation. So, in my case, your vision of the note would have read as follows: *The trenchless sanitary pipe rehabilitation scheduled on your block today, October 22, 2012, has been cancelled.* But—back to reality—there was no space on the note for a date after the comma. There were only two possibilities. One: You did not have the ability to translate your vision into reality, so I could not trust any efforts you might make to rehabilitate my sanitary pipes, trenchlessly or otherwise. Two: You were sloppy enough to insert a comma where it did not belong. How, then, could I trust you to be careful with my sewers? Both possibilities led to the same conclusion, one that did not bode well for you as a future service provider.

My next letter will be to the president of my condominium association. I wish I did not have to write that letter. But the maintenance of high standards is one hallmark of civilization and each of us has a role, however small, to play.

Sincerely,
Ariadne Jensen

To the president of Pharmabella from AJ

March 31, 2014

Dear Mr. Christopher,

I have been a customer at your Pharmabella stores for many years. On the odd occasion when I need prescription medications (and who does not, from time to time) I buy them at your pharmacy. I wear little makeup, but what I do purchase comes from Pharmabella. Soaps, cleaning supplies, and the occasional tasty treat, all Pharmabella merchandise. I don't know how many thousands of dollars I have spent at your stores over the years. I have watched (and in my own small way, helped) your company grow from a modest enterprise to a veritable retail giant. I do not keep track of such things but for all I know, you may be on the stock market.

I have always enjoyed a fine quality of product and good service at your stores. Until last Monday.

I went in to the store for one item: a pad of paper, the kind one writes letters on. In fact I am writing this letter on a sheet of paper from that pad.

You see, I write many letters—it is my passion—and for me to be without a pad of paper is like a smoker being out of cigarettes. Most of my letters are personal but from time to time I write to civic, provincial and federal politicians to let them know my thoughts on the issues of the day. On occasion, I write to businesspeople to inform them of pleasant or unpleasant events that have some connection with their enterprises. And that is the kind of letter I am writing you today.

When I found my way to the stationery department last Wednesday, I was disappointed that the pads of lovely vellum stock I prefer were sold out. There was only one pad of any kind left and, as you will see from examining the paper on which I am writing now, it was full of much plainer paper. But to be honest, in this email-dominated age of ours, I am grateful you carry letter pads at all.

The letter pad was on the top shelf. By raising myself to my full height and getting on to my toes, I was able to reach the item I needed. The store was slow at that hour and I brought it to the cash, intending to pay right away and leave without incident.

It was not to be.

The price tag on the back of the pad read $6.99 so with tax, the price should have been $7.34. (I have always been good at doing arithmetic in my head.) That was not what the cashier said to me. "Five eighty-seven," she said. I quickly calculated that the price was $5.59 plus tax, and that $5.59 is a twenty percent reduction from $6.99.

"Oh," I said, "there is a twenty percent sale on that pad?"

"Nope," the cashier said. "It's not on sale."

Then I realized what this all had to do with—the day of the week.

"You have given me the Pharmabella seniors' discount. Haven't you?" I said.

"You bet," the cashier said. "Every Monday."

"But I didn't ask for the discount."

"That's okay. I don't make other seniors ask either."

"So... you've simply assumed that I'm eligible."

"No problem, honey," she said.

Wanting more than anything to end the conversation, I opened my wallet. The cashier pointed out to me where in my wallet my Pharmabella points card was to be found. I was well aware of its location and needed no assistance.

"I often help older folks find the card," the cashier said, with pride in her voice. "You'd be surprised where some of them put it."

I paid. By now there was someone else in line at the cash. But the cashier was in no rush to get on with her job. Apparently, talking to me was more entertaining.

"The starting age is only sixty. And you are a spring chicken of—what—sixty-one?" she said. Then (and I am recounting the facts without embellishment), she winked.

As I was walking out of the store, she called, "Of course, you don't have to take the seniors' discount just 'cause you're old enough. But I've never had anyone turn it down yet!"

In spite of your cashier's certainty to the contrary, I can tell you I have not reached the magic age of sixty. I can see it, but I am not there. I did want to pay the regular price for my letterpad. But your cashier wore me down.

I like for people giving me service to conduct themselves in a civil, professional manner. Is that too much to ask?

I am disappointed in your company, in which I have put so much trust over the years. Do you not have a protocol that could be followed? If so, please enforce it. If not, please set one up. I would not like for your other customers to be subjected to the treatment I received.

Thank you for hearing me out.

Sincerely,
Ariadne Jensen

To the owner of the Café Versailles
from AJ—second letter

March 27, 2015

Dear Owner of the Café Versailles,

I hope this letter finds you in superlative health. My own health is at an acceptable level but unexceptional for a woman in her fifties. I will not trouble you with particulars. Suffice it to say I have learned over the years that both physical and mental health can benefit if a person takes a holiday or otherwise shifts her routine. Lately I have been feeling like I am in a rut, and of course, that perception can lead to loss of focus, despondency, and symptoms such as joint pain, for, as we all know, the knee bone is connected to the head bone.

I cannot let myself sink, I told myself. I am going to set out on some kind of adventure. Today. But as I am a woman of modest means, I will not be embarking on a cruise, checking into a spa, booking an all-inclusive. My adventure will need to be much less costly and, for that matter, less time-consuming, as I lead a busy life.

I was contemplating what form my adventure might take as I strolled into the Café Versailles shortly after two o'clock today for my customary mid-afternoon pick-me-up. I was about to order my usual small cappuccino, to which I had been looking forward for hours, when I saw a sign on the counter next to the till. The sign, which I had never noticed before, featured a photograph of a long-tailed, furry animal that looked like a cross between a raccoon and a cat. *The caption: Ask about our wild civet coffee.* So I did.

Your well-informed barista explained that the creature in the picture, the wild civet, consumes the cherries of the coffee plant and either regurgitates or poops out the beans, which are indigestible. The beans are cleaned by stout-hearted people and undergo further processing and, voilà, wild civet coffee. The barista said the effect of the civet's alimentary enzymes is such that the pooped coffee tastes nutty. Today, alas, none was available at the Versailles. However, the regurgitated variety, which tasted fruity, was on hand, and the barista would be pleased to brew me a cup.

Well, I thought to myself, this may well be the adventure I crave. Yes please, I said.

Then the barista told me the price. Twenty-five dollars. For one little cup of coffee? Yes, but not just any coffee. Exotic coffee—coffee that has been lovingly spat up in Thailand by a shaggy-haired creature. Well, at that price, I said, I suppose I can rest assured the beans were cleaned with extreme thoroughness. The barista laughed.

I watched her as she measured out the beans, ground them, and put the coffee on to brew. In a few minutes, it was ready. She poured it into a lovely white ceramic mug.

I found a table and took my first sip. Impossible. Second sip. Same experience. Then I downed the rest. I couldn't believe it. That coffee was, I can tell you without exaggeration, the blandest I have ever drunk. Completely tasteless.

So while my adventure did not cost me the earth or take a long time, I can't say it gave me the lift I so desired. I will not ask for a refund but I do think you should reconsider offering your customers wild civet coffee, especially at that fancy price.

And I wish you robust health.

Sincerely,
Ariadne Jensen

p.s. In fairness, I must admit I cannot speak to the pooped kind. I had only the regurgitated.

To the Tower II engineering technician at the Hotel Poseidon from AJ

October 12, 2013

Dear Engineering Technician:

Allow me to introduce myself as the individual who, earlier today, placed a small load of clothing into the dryer on top of which you find this note—Dryer #1. I emptied the lint filter, put my eight quarters into the slots, selected the permanent press setting, pushed the start button. Nothing happened. I assumed the dryer's failure to start was just a temporary thing, rather like the gap between the moment the conductor raises his baton and the moment the orchestra begins to play. However, the machine's music never did begin. Had I made a mistake? In view of the simplicity of the model—a feature I admire, as, most of today's appliances are too full of unnecessary options that only make the machines more susceptible to breakage—I did not think I had erred. Still, I reviewed. Lint filter emptied: check. Money properly inserted in and received by machine: check. Desired setting chosen and start button pushed: check and check.

I was prepared to give up and try Dryer #2, when a porter appeared in the hallway leading into the guest laundry room. I got his attention and he generously came to my aid. I saw from his badge that his name was Frank. I explained the situation and he had the perspicacity to do what I had not done—check the back of the machine. There he discovered a paper tag approximately the size of a business card on which was written, in small letters, the words "out of order."

"Oh gosh," Frank said. "I am so sorry. How are you supposed to see that?"

Frank said he would call the engineering department. He did so. He asked me to wait. In just a few minutes, he said, an engineering technician would come by and do whatever was required.

"But would it not make more sense for me to simply use Dryer #2?" I asked.

"Engineering will assist you," he said. And he repeated he was sorry.

"Really, there is no need to apologize," I said. "You've been nothing but helpful."

Frank said goodbye and walked back into the hall. Because I do not like to hurt anyone's feelings, I waited until I heard the elevator doors close, so that I could be confident Frank was on his way to his next destination. Then, I emptied the lint filter of Dryer #2, moved my load of laundry into it, placed my quarters into the slots, selected permanent press, and pushed the start button. Immediately, the dryer began to whir.

Despite what I told Frank, I actually have no intention of waiting for you, although if you do arrive here while I am writing this note (which is now turning into more of a letter), then of course I will be pleasant and will wish you well in your efforts to repair defective Dryer #1. But really, what purpose would be served by my waiting? I don't think Frank thought the situation through quite carefully enough. I have no expertise in dryer repair and can spend my time more profitably reading in my own room, Room 253, until it is time to retrieve my clothing from Dryer #2.

Since you are expected soon and it is likely we will miss each other, I would like to share a couple of items with you. First—if I may—a word of advice. Should you not repair Dryer #1 on this afternoon's visit, I would recommend you affix a sign to the front of the machine. The words "Out of Order" should be printed clearly in large letters, preferably with a felt-tipped pen. Until your baby gets fixed, you and I want the same thing: to spare other Poseidon guests the inconvenience and frustration of placing their clothes for drying in a machine that simply does not work. And I know Frank would want that too; indeed, I am sure he would say so if he were still here, standing stalwartly by my side in the laundry room.

The second matter is equally practical, but more delicate, as it concerns, well, money. According to the old adage, if someone says "It's not the money; it's the principle," it's the money. But that is not always so. Not when we are talking about two dollars. That is not a sum that will change my life. Still, it is a fact that after placing eight quarters in Dryer #1, I did not get what I had paid for. I hope and expect that someone representing the Hotel Poseidon will contact me before my departure tomorrow and make arrangements to reimburse me. Of course, you need not repay in quarters.

Sincerely,
Ariadne Jensen

LEO

Friendship, the highest form of love. No explanation possible. No justification required.

AJ

To Lady Gaga from AJ

April 2, 2012

Dear Stefani,

I know you prefer to be called by the name you have given yourself, but perhaps, under the circumstances, you will tolerate my addressing you as your parents do. If the article I just read is accurate, I believe you had a bad day today, and I would imagine you are quite upset. If you let me, I would like to help you recover. I hope you will take comfort in leaving celebrity behind for a few moments to read a note from somebody who cares for you as she would a daughter.

As it happens, I too had a bad day. I admit with embarrassment that my clumsy ways with technology played a large part. As you can see from this letter, my preferred tools for communication are pen and paper. I do send and receive email, but with a certain degree of reluctance—it simply does not carry the same value for me as handwritten correspondence. Email messages often strike me as rushed, lacking in depth, not well thought through. In any event, this morning, I received an email from someone whose name I did not recognize, but because of a tendency to trust people, I assumed there was a valid reason this individual had chosen to contact me. The email read like this: *We have important news about Lady Gaga. If you are over eighteen, click on the link below.* When I did, I found a message about you that was so vile, I will not repeat it to you. Within minutes, several friends alerted me to the fact that they had received the same message, through an email that had appeared to come from me, but had not. In short, I had been hacked, and consequently played an unintentional role in spreading a lie about you. I am so sorry. I spent the remainder of the day emailing everyone I know, one person at a time, with a personal note, an apology, and an assurance that the message about you was utterly false. I explained, as best I could, that I had been an innocent, if dimwitted, accessory to the smearing of your good name, and that in fact, I hold you in the highest regard.

If only we could find the one who started the attack. I fear we never will, given the ease with which people hide their identities in the Internet universe. I must learn to be more suspicious of communication that comes my way from strangers in this age of so-called connectedness. I am furious that someone has so viciously distorted your name and image.

My friend Leo tells me I should not take the incident so much to heart. Leo, who is in his twenties, knows the online cosmos well and does his best to explain it to me. He assures me the unpleasant event had nothing to do with either you or me personally. A phisherperson with issues was attempting to spread a virus, Leo says. Anyone's name could have been used as a lure, he says. But you and I know he has not paid enough attention to the human dimension of the problem. How would he feel if he were the one who'd been duped, as I was? Or if he had been used as the lure, as you were? And how would he feel if a malicious rumour were spreading all over the world wide web, not about you, but about him?

I would contend that through that hack, you and I were, in different ways, simultaneously hurt. And that makes me feel protective of you, dear Stefani, because I am much older than you and more accustomed to coming back from undeserved assaults. Feel free to lean a little.

Now, if I may, I will move on to discussion of the unpleasantness to which you were subjected today in your own city. If I have correctly understood the news item I just read, it seems that this afternoon, you were compelled to dismiss your choreographer, who had been loudly and widely proclaiming that she had created you, and in the image of Madonna. When a person says she has made another, she suffers from a goddess delusion. That choreographer deserves no credit for what you yourself have achieved. Moreover, you are one person and Ms Ciccone is another. Yes, you both perform in outré outfits. Many of Leo's contemporaries do the same, yet each is an individual. If that were not so, we'd have to conclude that every person who wears jeans is made in the image of some other person in jeans. Call me old school, but as I see it, when you pay a person to do a job for you, she owes you loyalty. In dismissing that choreographer earlier today, you acted justly. Yes, the choreographer is Canadian and I am Canadian, but that does not make what she did to you okay.

So this has not been a good day for either of us. For me, it has been challenging. For you, I fear, it has been one of too many difficult days. The verbal pummelling to which you are subjected is not only undeserved; it is constant. And what inane questions people throw at you. Whether you are a she or a he-she. Whether your dress is really made of meat. Perhaps your detractors, instead of cross-examining you, should ponder on the questions *you* ask. Such as, why did your fan Jamey die by his own hand at fourteen? Because he was gay and spoke out for tolerance, in spite of constant harassment? In advocating for Jamey, you advocate for so many others, including Leo. And I, for one, salute you for that.

Fifty percent of the world's population seem to understand you are an uncompromising artist and a fearless fighter for justice; regrettably, the other fifty percent are in cahoots with the ne'er-do-well who tricked me this morning (maligning you in the process) and the choreographer who treated you so badly this afternoon. As the young people say, you do you. I am with you, and so is Leo.

What a fine young adult you have turned into, Stefani. You want the return of the super-fan, you say. I hope you consider me qualified, for I am your oldest little monster.

Sincerely,
Ariadne Jensen

To Leo's mother from AJ

November 15, 2012

Dear Mrs. Ellison,

I am sorry I hung up on you yesterday. When a person shouts at me, I become rattled, sometimes to the point of what used to be called shell shock, and may actually lose the ability to talk.

Since you had three complaints and made each repeatedly, I saw no value in keeping the receiver glued to my ear. I do, however, have a strong dedication to courtesy and would at least have said goodbye if I had not temporarily lost the power of speech.

In any event, I am clear on your three points and am prepared to deal with them in turn now. If you do not mind, that is all I will do, and I do not expect a response. It would, in my opinion, be both unwise and unproductive for us to engage in ongoing correspondence.

Your first complaint is that Leo is twenty-two, while I am in my fifties and not his aunt or teacher, but rather, to use your words, "a complete stranger," and therefore, in your view, I must be a corrupting influence on Leo.

Let me assure you, the relationship between Leo and me is platonic. Even if that were not the case, the matter would be out of your hands, since your son is of age. However, I am no predator, and if I were to choose a romantic partner, that man would be considerably closer to my age. He would also be heterosexual.

That brings me to your second complaint—that Leo apparently tends to choose my company over yours. I would invite you to hearken back to your own early twenties. Who did you prefer to spend time with—your parents or your friends?

Your third complaint—and perhaps in a way it encompasses the first two—is that I have turned Leo against you. I cannot accept recognition for that. All credit for your son's alienation from you goes to one person, and that person is not I. Was it I who said to Leo, many times over, that same-sex sex is disgusting, a crime against nature, an abomination? Was it I who threw Leo out of the house when he arrived for Thanksgiving dinner because he was accompanied by his then-boyfriend? Do I try to break up not only Leo's romantic relationships, but also his friendships? Even if I wanted to, I could not contribute to turning Leo against you. There is nothing left to do.

As I have said, I do not think it necessary for us to communicate further. If, however, you find that you have more to say to me, and if you again select the telephone as your medium, please bear in mind that I have a thirty percent hearing loss in the left ear and so, as I am sure you can appreciate, exposure to screaming is detrimental to my health.

Sincerely,
Ariadne Jensen

To Leo's mother from AJ—second letter

February 28, 2013

Dear Mrs. Ellison,

How I wish it had not become necessary to write you again. It is not healthy for either of us to have contact with the other. However, since my attempt last November to explain the nature of the friendship between your son and me, your attitude toward me has not softened. That would not present a new problem in and of itself, but you have unfortunately gone further.

Leo tells me you have opened accounts on Facebook and Twitter with the express intent of casting aspersions upon my character in a public forum. He says you post comments at least twice a day—sometimes more frequently—in which you name me, describing me as a cougar, a self-styled milf, a Reverend-Moon or Jim-Jones type who has brainwashed Leo into liking me.

I wonder what you seek to accomplish by taking such strange measures. Having made several previous attempts, all unsuccessful, you must know by now that you cannot convince Leo to give me up as a friend. What then, can your motive be for your entry into the murky underworld of electronic slurs? Jealousy? Malice? Unadulterated hate?

I would invite you to reflect carefully on how you utilize your resources. Our days on earth are not long. Every time you decide to insult me on-line, you use up precious effort and time. How can your energy be channeled into a more constructive endeavour? You can, perhaps, volunteer for a worthwhile cause, such as your local food bank. Or you can enjoy daily strolls through a nature reserve with a field guide in your hand and learn to identify wildflowers. You can take up a hobby, such as tennis or calligraphy.

Any of those pursuits will turn you into a better person—and isn't that what we all want for ourselves? As a bonus, if you engage in one or more of the activities I have suggested, you will be too busy to think about me, and how I am, in your opinion, corrupting your son. As a consequence, you will stop making libelous posts about me on the Internet. And as a further, particularly happy consequence, I will not sue you for defamation.

The quest for self-improvement leads to a cornucopia of rewards, does it not, Mrs. Ellison.

Sincerely,
Ariadne Jensen

To Gregory Chudnovsky and David Chudnovsky from AJ

December 27, 2013

Dear Dr. Chudnovsky and Dr. Chudnovsky,
I find it enormously daunting to write this letter. How can a person of average intelligence have the temerity to communicate with the likes of you? And how can I expect you to attend to my words, even if I express myself succinctly? Yet I press on, for I believe even the briefest message from you may give a certain dispirited young student the boost he needs to continue with his studies. You see, he is a fan of yours; it is from him that I learned about you.

I refer to best friend Leo Ellison. He is in his early twenties while I am in my fifties. Some people, including his mother—particularly his mother—think our friendship makes no sense. However, I am certain you would not question our devotion to each other for a moment. Indeed, Doctors Chudnovsky, your insistence on working together throughout your adult lives, in spite of the resulting lost professional opportunities, causes me to believe that you do not think it anybody's business who keeps company with whom. Look at what the two of you have achieved together. Not just anyone could calculate pi to about a jillion digits, by using a homemade supercomputer that you kept from overheating through measurements taken with a meat thermometer. (I understand "pork" was the optimal temperature setting for the machine.) Who but the Brothers Chudnovsky could solve a wool–silk–and–silver–threaded medieval tapestry problem through the use of a vector displacement map and warping transformations (whatever those might be)? My point is, you have accomplished all these feats despite the challenges of starting a new life as emigrants to the United States when you were 26 and 31 years old, respectively, and also despite the fact that one of you suffers from the debilitating autoimmune neuromuscular illness myasthenia gravis.

Not only are you geniuses; you also know how to surmount adversity and carry on with important work.

I do not suggest that Leo is a genius. Still, he has much in common with you. He finds himself ostracized, for a couple of reasons. First of all, he is openly gay and in a particularly flamboyant way. Secondly, his best friend, with whom he spends a great deal of time, in settings both private and public, is a woman (me) frequently taken for his mother. To say some of his contemporaries are unkind to him is to severely understate the case. In fact they treat him with such contempt it is as though they themselves have never matured past a destructive, insensitive adolescence. Consequently, with only a few courses left to take until he finishes his bachelor's degree in political science with a minor in ancient history, Leo contemplates quitting university to join the work force. He simply wishes to escape the relentless taunting from his peers.

Personally, I would hate to see him give up. For one thing, I do not think the ostracism is any less likely to occur when Leo takes a job. He needs to develop the life skills to handle the bullies. I can help him with that, no matter what his situation. I have not applied myself to the task yet, and that has been my deficiency as a friend, but I intend to start on Operation Toughen-Leo-Up right away. However, it will take more convincing than I can single-handedly give to make him stick with his program of studies rather than running away.

Would you mind taking a few short minutes to write Leo a short note of encouragement? To make this small task more convenient for you, I have enclosed an envelope addressed to Leo and an international reply coupon which you can redeem for the postage required to mail your note from the United States to Canada.

I was elated to learn that after years of seeking academic positions that would suit the way you collaborate and the work you do, you secured positions on the faculty of the Polytechnic University in Brooklyn. I am certain that you can identify with Leo, and his sense of being an outsider. I am sure you also recognize it is essential for him to complete his first degree, and perhaps even advance academically, if he is to continue moving in a positive direction, as he so deserves to do. If anybody can convince him, it is you, Doctors Chudnovsky, for you are among his heroes.

Thank you for your serious consideration of my request.

Respectfully yours,
Ariadne Jensen

To Leo from AJ—second letter

August 14, 2012

Dear Leo,

Six weeks left until your return from your international summer school stay in Korea. Maybe you are better off being at Ajou University and nowhere around me right now. I am going through a period of feeling even more of a misfit than usual. If you were here you'd make me laugh about it.

You know I don't chase men. But I don't know... every once in a while, I see someone and am overwhelmed. At such times I think of my old gynecologist-obstetrician friend Harold, who said he always went about his business professionally but every two thousand patients or so he would internally examine a woman who he found, in spite of himself, alluring.

In any case, this morning I was in the coffee queue at that new downtown café, Swish, when a peculiar thing happened. In front of me stood a couple of men, talking to each other. One was probably a fine person and a credit to his family; to be honest, I neither knew nor cared. His companion, though. Oh, his companion. My my, what a fine example of manhood. From a strictly aesthetic point of view, I am convinced that if you and I had been together, you would have shared my admiration of him. He wore black pants, tailored and well-fitted without being excessively tight, and a spectacularly white shirt. He must have been a business executive, or perhaps, a waiter. What did I care? I was doomed.

A couple of minutes later, as we waited for our drinks near the pickup counter, I got a better look, as the beautiful one and his friend stood off to the right of me.

Height, five-nine. He'd look perfect by my side, especially if I were practicing posture-awareness like you always encourage me to do, and also if I were wearing those spunky patent-leather heels you convinced me to buy last June. Medium build with no flab in the middle. I caught a fantasy glance of him at his regular Saturday-morning racquetball match, looking godlike in his shorts and T-shirt and fingerless gloves.

Huge dark eyes, small nose and mouth. And could nature have made teeth so even? If not, I was prepared to call his mother and thank her for taking him, when he was a teen, to a great orthodontist.

He, mid-thirties. Me, fifties. He, sporting the telltale gold wedding band.

So what? Such things have been done before.

My drink was called, I picked it up, and when I turned around, he was gone. As far as I know, he had not even registered my presence.

Ending it that way was unfair to both of us. Let me rephrase that. Ending it that way was unfair to me.

But wait. Just like in Roy Orbison's song "Pretty Woman," he came back. He walked up to me, gently removed the coffee cup from my hand and placed it on the counter. Then he gathered me into his strong arms and gave me the kiss of my lifetime.

Not really. I had to make that last bit up as I sipped my coffee.

Take good care of yourself and keep enjoying your adventures in Korea.

Your devoted friend,
Ariadne

To Pope Francis from AJ—second letter

Calgary, Alberta
Canada
June 23, 2015

Your Holiness,
Not having received a response to my letter of January 16, I have hesitated to write you again with an update. However, I know you have been busy preparing your recently released no-nonsense encyclical on climate change, granting audiences to international leaders (even Mr. Putin), and discharging numerous other papal responsibilities. It is not easy, I am sure, to deal with all the correspondence that crosses your desk. Indeed, from what I understand—and my understanding is extremely imperfect—the curia is a complicated, even Byzantine bureaucracy. It is possible that my January letter sits unopened somewhere within the walls of the Vatican. And if that is the case, you are surely not at fault.

To avoid possibly needless repetition, however, I will assume you did receive my letter and have been meaning to respond. Your determination to do so is documented, I am sure, on your long pontifical to-do list. Do not trouble yourself, Your Holiness. I forgive you. And here is your update.

Gay-Straight Alliance clubs can now be set up in all schools where students want them. Catholic schools are included. This happy outcome is attributable partly to public pressure and partly to the work of a few enlightened politicians. There is no longer an urgent need for you to speak to the Bishop of Calgary or the Archbishop of Edmonton on the subject, although I would still recommend you keep an eye on them.

I know if you had time you would ask how Leo is doing. He is fine. As his best friend, I continue to share his hope that he will some day meet a nice man he can settle down with and start a family. I am well too, although I still have problems with Leo's mother, as does he. Perhaps I will write you about that one day. I would love to hear your take on the situation.

Until the next time, then.

Yours most respectfully,
Ariadne Jensen

Third letter to the CEO of Canada Post

July 11, 2015

Dear Mr. Chopra,

Congratulations on yesterday's issue of an Alice Munro stamp. This action is, of course, in the spirit of my own plan to save Canada Post, as outlined in my previous two letters. I see now that your failure to answer was more of a technicality, for you have clearly taken my basic message to heart.

So what we have here, at last, is a collaboration.

It has been my pleasure to inspire you. Rest assured I will keep sending you ideas. Together we will get the corporation back on its feet.

Sincerely,
Ariadne Jensen

p.s. I notice that in your announcement, you list a few of the awards Ms Munro has won over the years. However (and I am sure this is merely an oversight), you do not mention that she is a Nobel laureate. Please fix. Thank you.

Main sources

For Jenny Marx, Sophie Marx and Karl Marx:

Love and Capital: *Karl and Jenny Marx and the Birth of a Revolution,* by Mary Gabriel, Little, Brown & Company, 2011

The Letters of Karl Marx, selected and translated by Saul K. Padover, Prentice Hall, 1979

Karl Marx—Friedrich Engels, Selected Letters, The Personal Correspondence, 1844-1877, edited by Fritz J. Raddatz, translated from the German by Ewald Osers, Little, Brown, 1981

For Elizabeth Hall and John A. Macdonald:

Private Demons: The Tragic Personal Life of John A. Macdonald, by Patricia Phenix, McClelland and Stewart, 2006

Sir John A.: An Anecdotal Life of John A. Macdonald, edited by Cynthia Smith and Jack McLeod, Toronto, Oxford University Press Canada, 1989

John A., the Man Who Made Us: *The Life and Times of John A. Macdonald,* vol. 1, by Richard Gwyn, Random House Canada, 2007

For Helen Keller and Peter Fagan:

The World I Live In, by Helen Keller, edited and with introduction by Roger Shattuck, The New York Review of Books, 2003 (originally written in 1908)

The Story of My Life, by Helen Keller, Grosset & Dunlap, c. c. 1902, 1903, 1905

Midstream, by Helen Keller, 1929, reprinted by Greenwood Press, 1968

Helen & Teacher: The Story of Helen Keller and Anne Sullivan Macy, by Joseph P. Lash, Radcliffe Biography Series, Delacorte Press, 1980

Helen Keller, Courage in Darkness, by Emma Carlson Berne, Sterling, 2009

Helen Keller: A Life, by Dorothy Herrmann, Albert A. Knopf, 1999

Helen Keller in Love, by Rosie Sultan, Viking, 2012

FOR RUTH DRAPER AND LAURO DE BOSIS:

The World of Ruth Draper: A Portrait of an Actress, by Dorothy Warren, Southern Illinois University Press, 1999

The Art of Ruth Draper, Her Dramas and Characters, by Ruth Draper, edited by Morton Dauwen Zabel, with a memoir by Morton Dauwen Zabel, Oxford University Press, 1960

The Letters of Ruth Draper, 1920–1956, A Self-Portrait of a Great Actress, edited with narrative noted by Neilla Warren, Charles Scribner's Sons, 1979

FOR RABINDRANATH TAGORE AND ANAPURNA TURKHUD:

Rabindranath Tagore: The Myriad-Minded Man, by Krishna Dutta and Andrew Robinson, Bloomsbury, 1995

Modern Indian Responses to Religious Pluralism, edited by Harold G. Coward, State University of New York Press, 1987

Gitanjali: A Collection of Prose Translations made by the Author from the Original Bengali, by Rabindranath Tagore, copyright 1913 by MacMillan Publishing Company, copyright renewed 1941 by Rabindranath Tagore, First Scribner Poetry Edition, 1997

FOR HELENA JANS AND RENÉ DESCARTES:

Descartes: The Life and Times of a Genius, by A.C. Grayling, Walker & Company, 2007

Cogito, Ergo Sum: The Life of René Descartes, by Richard Watson, David R. Godine, Publisher, 2002

thecaveonlinecom/APEH/17THcenturymedicineDBQ.html

FOR ANNA MARIA MOZART AND MARIA THERESIA HAGENAUER:

Mozart's Women, by Jane Glover, Macmillan, London, 2005

Mozart's Letters, Mozart's Life, edited and translated by Robert Spaethling, Norton, 2000

FOR JAMES WOLFE AND HENRIETTA WOLFE:

The Life of Major-General James Wolfe, founded on Original Documents and Illustrated by his Correspondence, by Robert Wright, Chapman and Hall, London, 1893 (Google e-book)

Wolfe at Quebec: The Man Who Won the French and Indian War, by Christopher Hibbert, Cooper Square Press, 1999

Paths of Glory: the Life and Death of General James Wolfe, by Stephen Brumwell, McGill-Queen's University Press, 2006

For Hermann Einstein and Albert Einstein:

Einstein: The Life and Times, by Ronald W. Clark, Harper Perennial, HarperCollins. First Avon Books edition published 1972; First Harper Perennial edition published 2007

The Private Albert Einstein, by Peter A. Bucky in collaboration with Allen G. Weakland, Andrews and McMeel, A Universal Press Syndicate Company, 1992

Einstein: The Enduring Legacy of a Modern Genius, Writer/Editor Richard Lacayo, © Time Entertainment Inc., 2011

Albert Einstein, The Human Side: New Glimpses from his Archives, selected and edited by Helen Dukas and Banesh Hoffmann, © the Estate of Albert Einstein, Princeton University Press, 1979

For Jane Barker and Aphra Behn:

"Jane Barker and her Life (1652-1732): The Documentary Record," by Kathryn R. King and Jeslyn Medoff, *Eighteenth Century Life* 21 (November 1997): 16-38@1998 by the Johns Hopkins University Press

The Passionate Shepherdess: Aphra Behn 1640-89, by Maureen Duffy, Methuen, Great Britain, 1989 (first published in Great Britain 1977 by Jonathan Cape Ltd.)

For Esther Brandeau and Catherine Churiau:

Dictionary of Canadian Biography,
http://www.biographi.ca/en/index.php

"The Strange Story of Esther Brandeau, The First Jewish Arrival in Canada," by Isidore Goldstick, *The Canadian Jewish Chronicle*, Sept. 14, 1945:

https://news.google.com/newspapers?nid=883&dat=19450914&
id=q_9OAAAAIBAJ&sjid=dUwDAAAAIBAJ&pg=6736,515512
2&hl=en

For Aristides de Sousa Mendes:

"Aristides de Sousa Mendes," by Maria Julia Cirurgiao and
Michael D. Hull, Jewish Virtual Library, http://www.jewishvir-
tuallibrary.org/jsource/biography/Mendes.html, originally published in Lay Witness, October, 1998

"The Righteous Among the Nations: The Insubordinate Consul:
Aristides de Sousa Mendes, Portugal," Yad Vashem, http://www.
yadvashem.org/yv/en/righteous/stories/mendes.asp

"Aristides de Sousa Mendes: His Life and Legacy, Sousa Mendes
Foundation, http://sousamendesfoundation.org/aristides-de-
sousa-mendes-his-life-and-legacy/

For Charlotte Whitton:

The Canadian Encyclopedia
www.thecanadianencylopedia.ca

"Canadian Jews against planned honours for former mayor of
Ottawa,"www.worldjewishcongress.org/en/news/canadian-
jews-against-planned-honors-for-former-mayor-of-Ottawa

"City Drops Whitton name from archives plan, CBC News
Ottawa, May 9, 2011, www.cbc.ca

For Golda Meir:

Golda, by Elinor Burkett, HarperCollins, 2008

FOR DEREK WRAGGE-MORLEY:

The Ant World, by Derek Wragge-Morley, Penguin, London, 1953

FOR PEG WOFFINGTON:

Ladies First: The Story of Woman's Conquest of the British Stage, by W. Macqueen-Pope, W.H. Allen, 1952

FOR EMILIE DU CHÂTELET:

Passionate Minds, by David Bodanis, Crown Publishers, 2006

La Dame d'Esprit, by Judith P. Zinnsser, Viking Penguin, 2006

FOR VINCENZIO VIVIANI, JACOPO PANZANINI, AND GALILEO GALILEI:

Galileo's Daughter, by Dava Sobel, Walker & Company, 2011 edition

"Post-Galilean Thought and Experiment in Seventeenth-Century Italy: The Life and Work of Vincenzio Viviani," by Luciano Boschiero, History of Science, xliii (2005), 79-100

FOR XANTHIPPE AND ASPASIA:

Socrates: A Man for Our Times, by Paul Johnson, Viking, 2011

Socrates: A Life Examined, by Luis E. Navia, Prometheus Books, 2007

"The Ancient Greek Calendar," polysyllabic.com, ww.polysyllabic.com/?q=calhistory/earlier/greek

For Joseph Pujol:

"Le Pétomane Joseph Pujol," 1973 You Tube https://www.youtube.com/watch?v=M8pGUZLF6_o

"Professional Farters," Article #56, by Joseph Bellows, http://www.damninteresting.com/professional-farters/

For Gregory Chudnovsky and David Chudnovsky:

"The Mountains of Pi," by Richard Preston, *The New Yorker*, March 2, 1992

"Profile: Brothers Chudnovsky, PBS Nova science Now: 9 – Profile: Brothers Chudnovsky, https://www.youtube.com/watch?v=PsW2lYVU020

Acknowledgments

I respectfully acknowledge that I wrote this book on Treaty 7 territory, traditional lands of First Nations and Métis peoples.

Some letters in the book have appeared previously in *The Copperfield Review, The Prairie Journal of Canadian Literature,* and the anthology *Freshwater Pearls Online* (Alexandra Writers' Centre Society). Thank you to the editors of those publications.

Thank you to these people:
Filomena Gomes, for conversations on Aristides de Sousa Mendes.
Roberta Rees, for conversations on Esther Brandeau and voice.
Madelaine Shaw Wong, for conversations on Brandeau and the Catholic religion.
Betty Jane Hegerat, for reassurance that the book had legs.
The Louise Riley Library staff, for friendliness and a great workspace.
Chris Needham and Now Or Never Publishing, for belief in the book.

Without my family's unflagging encouragement, patience, and love, I would not have written this book or anything else. Bill Paterson, Lucy Altrows, Grace Paterson, Oliver Evans, Irwin Altrows—you have my gratitude and love.